MYSTERY OF THE
EMPTY HOUSE

(Original title: *Secret of the Old Post Box*)

by DOROTHY STERLING

Illustrated by June Goldsborough

SCHOLASTIC BOOK SERVICES

NEW YORK • LONDON • RICHMOND HILL, ONTARIO

Other books by the same author
available through Scholastic Book Services:
Mary Jane
Silver Spoon Mystery

This book is sold subject to the condition that it shall not be resold, lent, or otherwise circulated in any binding or cover other than that in which it is published—unless prior written permission has been obtained from the publisher—and without a similar condition, including this condition, being imposed on the subsequent purchaser.

Text copyright © 1960 by Dorothy Sterling. Illustrations copyright © 1968 by Scholastic Magazines, Inc. This edition is published by Scholastic Book Services, a division of Scholastic Magazines, Inc., by arrangement with Doubleday and Company, Inc.

1st printing .... January 1968

Printed in the U.S.A.

CONTENTS

1. A Telephone Call 7

2. Bat Meets Ball 14

3. I'm Not Scared 20

4. Ghosts and Girls 26

5. Making Friends 36

6. The Man in the Kitchen 44

7. Pre-posterous! 51

8. Mr. Popham Talks 57

9. Nathaniel Woodruff's Letter 63

10. Behind the Bricks 74

11. If I Were Nathaniel Woodruff 84

12. Treasure Hunting 93

13. The Missing Fireplaces 100

14. Listen! 107

15. The Book and Other Treasures 115

16. Alphabet Soup 125

17. I Care About Old Books 132

18. Master Spy or Master Thief? 140

19. A Smile from Nat 149

20. Note to the Reader 159

MYSTERY OF THE
EMPTY HOUSE

1 | A Telephone Call

THE SUN WAS SHINING in Pat's eyes. She squinted and pulled the pillow over her face, trying to go back to sleep. But that was crazy, because there was never any sun in her bedroom. Half awake, she tried to figure it out.

Suddenly she sat up and looked around, tossing her pillow across the room. And then she remembered: she wasn't in a gloomy New York apartment any more. The family had moved to Haven, where the sun shone in the morning and the birds sang. She could hear a regular chorus of them now, singing as if they were in a Disney nature film on TV.

Kneeling on a paper carton, she looked out of the window. There were still puddles everywhere from

7

yesterday's rain, but today was warm and bright and the air smelled fresh.

She wondered what time it was. The clock on her desk wasn't plugged in, and she hadn't the slightest idea where Mother had packed her watch. It must be early though, because not another soul was stirring. Only Pat and the birds were awake.

From the window she could see all the way down New Street to the Old Post Road. New Street wasn't really new. It was one of the oldest streets in Haven, Daddy said. But because it was a mile or two away from the stores and station, not many people lived on it.

Across the street there was a house almost exactly like the Harrisons'. If she leaned over to one side, she could read the sign out front that said GRAY. Daddy knew the Grays because he used to live in Haven when he was a boy. Down at the corner there was a little stone cottage all covered with vines. A funny little building with a wavy green roof, it made Pat think of the gingerbread house in *Hansel and Gretel.*

That was all, unless you counted the Haunted House. The Haunted House wasn't exactly on New Street. Or on any other street for that matter. It was way back from the road, separated from Pat's yard by a tumbledown stone wall and a field covered with brambles and tall grass.

Probably it wasn't really haunted, but Pat called it that because it was so old and dilapidated. From the front it was a regular two-story house, but in the back its roof sloped almost all the way down to the ground. Its shutters hung from the windows at crazy angles, and its clapboard walls looked as if they hadn't seen paint for a hundred years. Someday soon, when she'd had her fill of biking and tree climbing, Pat planned to explore the Haunted House and see what it was like inside.

Turning from the window, she decided to get dressed and go out. Nothing was properly unpacked yet, and she had to rummage through two cartons and a half-emptied barrel before she found a shirt and shorts and a pair of dry shoes. By this time her room looked as if a tornado had struck.

"Pat, oh Pat! Time for breakfast," Mother was calling.

Pat tried to tiptoe down the stairs, pretending that she hadn't heard, but it was no use. Dad was in the bathroom shaving, and Mother was in the kitchen. There was no way to get past them without being seen. So it was, "Pat, set the table, please," "Pat, find the sugar," and "Pat, I want you to help your mother today."

9

Mother thought of all sorts of ways for Pat to help. When Grandma came, soon after Daddy left for work, *she* thought of ways too. Neither of them would even stop to listen to Pat's own plans for the day.

Pat pouted as she dumped wastebaskets and carried paper cartons to the garage. She frowned as she hung her dresses in her closet, and grumbled as she put her socks and sweaters away. But by the time she reached the box of books and games, she felt in a good humor again.

There was room for all the books on the shelves above the desk, and room for all the games on the shelves beside the window. Not stacked on top of each other either, but spread out, so that you could see which was parcheesi and which was checkers without having to hunt through a whole pile.

Her dolls were at the bottom of the box. There was the diapered baby who had lived through a million games of "house"; the princess doll with a blue silk dress and pearl necklace, who was much too pretty to be played with; and last of all, long-legged, floppy Emily. The baby and the princess went on the shelf next to the games, but Emily had always belonged on the bed.

Pat arranged her carefully on the bedspread that

Grandma had made, and then stood back to study the effect. Somehow Emily didn't look quite right on the new striped bedspread in the new sunny room. Was it, could it possibly be, that at eleven she was too old for dolls?

While she was pondering this, the telephone rang.

"It's for you, Patricia," Grandma called up the stairs.

"For me?" Who in the world could be calling her? Outside of Grandma, she didn't know a single soul in Haven.

"This is Jim Gray," a hesitant voice at the other end of the line explained. "I live across the street, and my mother said I had to call you. I mean, she knows your father, and she said . . ."

Pat could hear a grownup in the background, prompting him. "I mean," Jim continued, "how would you like to play ball with us? We haven't got a real team — just four boys — but . . ."

Again the grownup voice said something.

"We'd like very much to have you play with us," Jim finished quickly.

"Okay." Pat couldn't think of anything else to say. "What . . . where'll I meet you?" she stammered after a long pause.

"The field behind your house. Half an hour." Now that everything was settled, Jim sounded more confident. "Bring along any equipment that you have."

"Equipment?" What did he mean?

"Ball, bat, mitt, whatever you've got. G'by." And Jim hung up.

Putting down the phone, Pat walked slowly into the kitchen. "That was Jim Gray," she announced. "Boy across the street. He asked me to play ball with him. With four boys, in fact."

"That's nice, dear." Her mother smiled absent-mindedly. "Better run up and change your clothes before you go."

Pat looked down at her rumpled shorts and scratched her head.

"Your green pedal pushers," Mother suggested.

"They look nice." Grandma agreed.

Pat trudged upstairs slowly. What on earth *did* you wear to play ball with a bunch of boys? Mothers and grandmothers were supposed to know about these things, but maybe they were wrong. And what *did* you talk to boys about, anyway? If you had gone to a girls' school all your life and never had a brother or even a boy cousin, you couldn't help wondering. Pat wasn't scared exactly, but, well, she couldn't help wondering.

Somewhere among the games on the shelf by the window there was a red rubber ball. She bounced it against the wall, caught it, bounced it again. Then she tried "One-two-three-O'Leary." After she'd counted up to a hundred without missing once, she felt better.

"Fiddlesticks," she scolded herself. "I'm pretty good at playing ball. Besides, boys are just the same as girls — or almost the same anyway."

Having decided this, she brushed her hair, changed into her pedal pushers and the new green blouse that matched, and stuffed the ball into her pocket. She turned for a last look at her room.

"Boys are almost the same as girls," she repeated out loud. But before she went downstairs, she lifted long-legged, floppy Emily from her place on the striped bedspread and stretched her out on the shelf behind the parcheesi set.

"Have a good time playing ball," Mother called as Pat ran out the back door.

"I will," Pat called back.

But she didn't.

2 | Bat Meets Ball

It wasn't Jim's fault, Pat had to admit. As soon as he saw her climbing over the wobbly stone wall at the back of her yard, he ran over to her.

"Hi," he said. "I'm Jim Gray. Come on and meet the others." He even put out his hand to shake hers, as if they were at a party or something.

Pat looked sideways at him as they walked across the field. He was about her age, with red-brown hair and a sprinkling of freckles on his nose. Not handsome exactly, but nice.

The others were stretched out on the grass, with a pile of mitts and a bat alongside them. When Jim and Pat approached, they sat up and stared. Stared as if they'd never seen anything like Pat in their whole lives before.

Pat stared back. Except that they were different sizes, they looked exactly alike. Each boy had straight black hair, round black eyes, and dead-white skin. And each boy was scowling.

"This is Patricia Harrison." Jim introduced her. "Nathaniel, Jonathan, and Samuel Paine." He pointed to the boys one by one.

"Hello." Pat smiled.

The Paines continued to stare and continued to scowl. At last the biggest one, the one named Nathaniel, threw down the piece of grass which he had been sucking.

"Patricia!" He turned on Jim. "You said 'Pat.' You didn't say a word about a *girl*."

"Didn't say a word about a boy either." Jim grinned. "Besides, I bet she can play as well as Sam."

"Can *not*." The smallest Paine, who looked as if he wasn't even seven, brushed back a lock of hair from his eyes.

"Don't care how well she plays. She can't play with *us*," Nathaniel said.

"Right." Jonathan nodded.

"Right," Sam agreed.

"She can too play." Jim calmly contradicted them. "You know perfectly well we need her. This way we can have somebody in the field besides the pitcher and —"

"But not a *girl,*" Nathaniel insisted.

"Not a *girl,*" Jonathan echoed.

"Not a *girl,*" Sam squeaked.

It was almost funny, the way they kept on talking about her as if she weren't standing there. Pat turned on her heel and headed for home. She hadn't gone far before Jim overtook her.

"I'm sorry," he apologized. "The Paines — well, you have to get to know them. Once you know them, they're really okay."

"They're pains, all right." Pat raised her voice so that it would carry across the field. "Big fat pains in the neck."

"Come on back," Jim urged.

"And play with them? Never." Pat took another step toward the stone wall.

Jim sighed. "It's only Nat. Ever since he got to be twelve and went to junior high, he thinks he has to hate girls. In junior high, you either get silly about girls and take them to the movies or you hate them. Johnny and Sam don't care. They just copy him because he's the oldest."

Pat hesitated. "But they won't let me play anyway," she argued.

"They'll let you." Jim sounded as if he knew what he was talking about. "They have to."

Reluctantly she trailed him to the trio on the grass. She really wanted to go home, but she guessed that she'd better give the Paines one more try.

"She's playing," Jim announced in a voice of authority.

"Who says?" Nat challenged him.

"I do. And I'll give you two good reasons why." Jim ticked them off on his fingers as he talked. "One, my mother said so — and yours would too if she knew about it. Two, it's my bat. No Pat, no bat. No bat, no game."

The Paines thought it over for a moment. Clearly, Jim had won the argument. Nat uncrossed his legs and stood up. Brushing off the seat of his dungarees, he reached for a mitt.

"I'll take Sam," he said, "and you can have Johnny and her. Shoot you for first ups."

"Right." Jim nodded.

Right? Nothing was right for Pat that day. Her pedal pushers were too tight in the knees when she ran. The bat was too heavy and the ball too hard. She had been pretty good at baseball in the school gymnasium in New York, but now she was stumbling and fumbling as if she didn't know how to play.

Nat snickered at her underhand throwing style. Johnny groaned when she let an easy fly slip through her fingers. Sam chortled when she swung at a ball that was far too low.

Even Jim looked troubled as she came up to bat again. "Wait him out," he whispered. "He'll get rattled. Let him walk you."

For a moment Pat thought of taking his advice. But when Nat winked at his brothers as he wound up for the pitch, she changed her mind. Resting the bat on her shoulder, she crouched low over the plate, the way she had seen the boys do. The first throw was high over her head, but she swung anyway.

"Strike one," Sam gleefully announced.

The second throw was low and she missed it. "Strike two."

This was it, her last chance. When the ball floated toward her, she tightened her fingers on the bat. Then she swung with all her might. She heard a resounding "thwack" as bat met ball.

"Run!" Jim shouted. "It's a beauty."

Pat tossed down the bat, hitched up her pedal pushers, and ran.

3 | I'm Not Scared

First base, second base, third. With her head high, Pat trotted across the burlap bag which marked home plate. She had hit a homer, the very first homer in her life. *Now* the boys would be less scornful of her ballplaying!

But the boys weren't there. When she looked around for approval, she saw all four of them standing near the Haunted House, yelling at each other. Or were they yelling at her? Because her hit, her beautiful home-run hit, had sailed across the field. It had sailed through the trees and right into a window of the old house.

Nat led the angry quartet back to the field. Throwing his mitt down in front of Pat, he shouted, "Now see what you've done!"

"Spoiled the game," Johnny accused.

"Your fault," Sam said.

Pat turned to Jim. "Did — did I break the window?"

"Ncpe." He glumly shook his head. "That's the one that was broken ages ago. But the ball — it's our only ball."

"Now we can't play any more." Nat flopped on the grass.

Relieved to hear that at least the window wasn't her fault, Pat fished her red rubber ball from the pocket of her pedal pushers. As soon as she had done it, she knew that it was a mistake. "I don't suppose . . . I mean . . . we couldn't use this?"

There was a chorus of groans, but no one even bothered to answer. Gosh, they didn't have to be so mean about it. After all, it wasn't as if she'd lost the ball on purpose. Besides —

"Let's go hunt for the ball," she proposed. "Inside the house."

Jim looked at Nat inquiringly. Nat shook his head. Johnny shook his head. Sam shook his head. The silence was thick enough to be cut with a knife.

Pat felt herself getting red from her neck all the way to the tips of her ears. It took a lot to make her angry, but now she was mad, mad clear through.

"You're scared." She challenged them. "Afraid the house is haunted."

"Not scared," Jim answered at last, "Just . . . well, we promised . . . we promised never to go into that house."

"Well, *I* didn't promise." Pat tossed her head. "I'm not scared. I'll go in and find your dirty old ball for you."

She flounced away from them. What was that word the boys in the park used when they were angry at each other?

"You're chicken." She turned to shout. "You're just a bunch of chickens, every single one of you."

Jim caught up with her as she tramped across the field. "Don't go," he begged. "I'll ask my mother to take us downtown later, and we can buy another ball."

"I'm going." Pat raised her chin defiantly. "Tell me why I shouldn't."

"The Paines . . . it's a secret," he stammered. "I can't tell you."

"Then I'll tell you. I'm sick of the Paines." Pat exploded. "I may not be the best ballplayer in the world, but I'm *not scared*. Not of Paines or ghosts or anything. *And I'm going to get that ball.*"

Jim shrugged his shoulders and left her to trudge on alone. The tall grass came to an end abruptly,

and she entered a cleared area. First, there was sort of an orchard where green apples bobbed from the branches of crooked old trees. Then an arbor, heavy with grapevines. And beyond that the remains of a formal garden. In spite of the weeds, there were flowers in bloom — blue ones and pink ones, whose names Pat didn't know, and an enormous scarlet rosebush which straggled up the side of the house.

"Even the garden looks haunted," she said out loud.

Her voice sounded strange in the deserted garden. She was beginning to feel a little less mad and a little more scared. After all, if those boys who had lived on New Street all their lives wouldn't go into the house — well, there just might be a reason why.

Pursing her lips, she studied the side of the house. Three windows on the first floor, two on the second, and a little one under the roof. It was easy to guess where the ball had entered, because all of the windows had panes and shutters except one. The ground-floor window next to the rosebush was glassless, shutterless — and dark.

Pat glanced back over her shoulder toward the baseball field. The three Paines and Jim were standing where she had left them. They were watching, waiting to see if she dared to enter the house.

The window was low, and it was easy to boost

herself up to the sill. For a moment she straddled it, one leg in and one leg out. For a moment she looked up at the sun and smelled the roses and listened to the buzzing of the bees. Then she swung her other leg over and faced the dark room. It smelled musty, and she could hear creaky, squeaky noises.

Her heart beat faster, as she thought about mice and spiders, and perhaps even a little bit about ghosts. Again she turned to see if the boys were still watching. They were. Well, there was no use putting it off any longer. She'd have to jump.

It was like plunging into deep water for the first time in summer, when you aren't sure if you still remember how to swim. Worse really, because when you jump into the water, at least you can see where you are going.

Thinking about jumping into the water gave her an idea. She held her nose and slowly counted.

"One chimpanzee. Two chimpanzees. Three."

When she got up to the third chimpanzee, she jumped from the window into the room. She jumped, only to land a second later on something squirmy and squashy and soft. Something that howled. Something that moaned. *Something* that plainly said "Ouch!"

4 | Ghosts and Girls

Pat ROLLED OVER ON THE FLOOR, too terrified to move. She could hear quick, short breaths and the "thump, thump" of a heart. Was it her own heart and breathing? Or did it belong instead to the squirmy soft something alongside her?

"Gosh," a high-pitched voice complained. "Why don't you look where you're going?"

Pat blinked and sat straight up. As her eyes grew accustomed to the dim light in the room, she could make out a shadowy shape. It wasn't a ghost. It was a real live person.

"Who are you?" Pat asked in a shaky voice.

"I'm a new girl," the shadow replied. "Name's Patricia Harrison."

The hair on the back of Pat's neck stood up straight. This was crazy. She was hearing things that didn't make any sense. She reached out and grabbed the shadow's shoulder and shook it — hard. All the exasperation of the afternoon went into that shake.

"You can't be." She exploded. "Because *I* am. My—name—is—Patricia—Harrison—and—I—live—on—New—Street—in—Haven."

She emphasized each word with another shake, until the stranger was rocking back and forth. Rocking back and forth with laughter.

Pat's hands dropped into her lap. This was getting more like a dream every minute. Pretty soon she would wake up and discover that she was still in the apartment in New York.

"Who *are* you?" she demanded to know.

Between giggles, her companion answered. "I'm really Barbara Thomas. I live at the other end of town, next door to your grandmother. She's been telling me about your moving here and —"

"But why did you say you were me?" Pat tried to sound stern, although the corners of her mouth were beginning to twitch.

Barbara shrugged her shoulders and spread out her hands, as if to say, "Who knows?" "Everybody

27

on my street's in camp or visiting somewhere, so I thought I'd bike over to meet you. Then, when I saw you all playing ball, I decided to come in here and look around. I always did like this house."

"But . . ." Pat still didn't understand.

"I was just going to climb out the window again when I heard someone coming in. So I ducked, naturally. Then you landed on top of me and asked who I was, and I said the first name that came into my head, naturally." Barbara burst into giggles again.

"Naturally." Even Pat laughed this time.

"I certainly did meet you," Barbara pointed out.

"You certainly did," Pat agreed. Putting out her hand, she gave Barbara's a vigorous tug. "How do you do, Miss Thomas? Charmed, I'm sure."

The two girls stood up and began to brush the cobwebs from their clothes. In the light from the window, they looked each other over. Barbara was tiny, with short brown hair and bright, birdlike eyes. She wasn't much bigger than Sam Paine.

Pat couldn't keep from sounding disappointed, as she blurted, "But you're only a little girl!"

"Eleven. Same as you. Your grandmother told me."

"What I meant was . . . you're so . . ." Pat began to flounder. "I guess you haven't really started growing yet."

"What you mean" — Barbara corrected her with a grin — "is that I'm a shrimp. My father says that the only thing big about me is my mouth."

Pat studied her face. "Your mouth isn't big," she answered politely.

"He means I talk too much," Barbara explained.

Just then they heard a voice outside the window. "G-i-ve me b-a-a-ck my ba-a-ll," the voice quavered.

Both girls jumped; even Barbara was speechless for a moment. Then she leaned on the sill and began to scold. "I see you, Jim Gray. What's the idea of trying to frighten us?"

"Only way I could get a word in." Jim's smiling face emerged into view. "I thought you were going to find the ball, Pat."

Guiltily, Pat began to look around. The ball was on the far side of the room. Picking it up, she handed it through the window to Jim.

"Sorry," she apologized. "I forgot all about it."

"No wonder, with Barbara talking. When you get tired of listening, come on back and join the game." With a wave of his hand, he was gone.

"You want to play with them?" Barbara asked.

"It's perfectly all right with me if you want to play with them."

Pat made a "fooey" noise with her lips. "Of course I don't want to play with them. I never in my whole life met anyone so mean as those Paines."

"You have to get to know them," Barbara explained. "Once you get to know them, they're really okay. It's only Nat. Ever since he got to be twelve —"

"— and went to junior high, he thinks he has to hate girls." Pat finished for her.

"My mother says it's only a stage boys go through, and not to pay attention." Barbara nodded. "It used to be fun to come over here. Until the last few months, really. Until they lost it for taxes, you know."

Pat didn't know, and she wasn't sure if she wanted to. "Lostitfortaxes" sounded like the name of a terrible sickness, and while she didn't exactly wish it on Nat Paine or his brothers, still she was pretty sick of them.

"This room" — she tried to change the subject — "what is it anyway?"

"It's the kitchen, silly. Can't you see?"

Pat leaned back against the window sill. She could see a little. Enough to make out a low ceiling, with broad beams running the length of the room, and an enormous brick fireplace which took up most of the opposite wall. A kitchen? It certainly didn't look like the kitchen in the Harrisons' new house. And yet it seemed familiar somehow.

She scratched her head, puzzled. "I have the funniest feeling that I've seen it before."

"Maybe." Barbara nodded. "Lots of people have. Including George Washington and Lafayette. And me. My father says they ought to make it into a museum and then put up a sign: *Barbara Thomas Slept Here*."

"That's it." Pat snapped her fingers.

"What's it?"

"A museum. That's exactly where I saw it — in a museum."

"Not this room," Barbara argued. "This has been here practically forever. Since before the American Revolution. It's the very oldest house in Haven."

"Not this room," Pat agreed, "but one almost like it. Only that one had pots and things hanging in the fireplace, and a spinning wheel and a warming pan and —"

"They had a spinning wheel and a warming pan too," Barbara interrupted. "We used it one night when I was sleeping here. Only it scorched the sheets, and Mrs. Paine was awfully mad."

31

"Mrs. Paine? You mean the same Paines as those boys?" Pat jerked her thumb in the direction of the ballplayers.

"Uh huh." Barbara nodded. "This house was built by their great-great — I forget how many greats — grandfather."

"Well, if it's their house, why don't they live here?"

"That's just the trouble," Barbara explained. "That's really why Nat's so mean. My mother says we shouldn't get angry at him. He used to boast all the time, 'cause George Washington slept here and Lafayette, and now they're all crowded into that tiny house with the three of them sleeping in one room."

George Washington, Lafayette, and Nat Paine all sleeping in one room? Pat's head was beginning to spin.

"Ever since their father was killed in the war, things went wrong for their family," Barbara continued. "Until now they're losing it for taxes."

Hopelessly entangled, Pat managed to squeeze in a question. "The war? You mean the American Revolution?"

Barbara groaned. "The Korean War, silly. But there were Paines killed in the Revolution, I guess, and British soldiers occupied the house for a while, and they —"

"Whoa, Dobbin!" Pat hoisted herself up to the window sill and swung her feet. "I'm about a mile behind you. You mean that it's because of the British that those boys don't live here any more?"

Barbara gulped. "Told you I talked too much. I'll try to explain. The Paines always lived here, even since before the Revolution. Then Nat Paine's father — he was Johnny and Sam's father too — got killed in a plane in Korea. Mrs. Paine had to go to work. She's a nurse, and you know how much money nurses make. She just didn't have enough to paint the house or fix things when they got broken, or even pay the taxes. She owed so much taxes that finally, last winter, the town council told her she'd have to pay up or they'd sell the house."

"How can they do that?" Pat asked. "I mean, if it belongs to the Paines."

"They're doing it." Barbara shrugged her shoulders. "The house still belongs to the Paines, but in August the town is going to sell it at auction. August fifteenth. My father says it's a shame. He tried to get people to raise money to pay the taxes for Mrs. Paine, but he couldn't. They wouldn't, that is. He says people in Haven are a bunch of rock-ribbed, rugged individualists who wouldn't help their own grandmas."

"But why don't the boys live here now? Till August fifteenth, anyway?"

"Furnace," Barbara explained. "It stopped working right after the town council said they were going to take the house anyway. No heat, no hot water. So instead of waiting, the Paines moved to that little house at the corner. That belongs to them too. It used to be the gatehouse long ago, when the Paines owned everything on New Street. Only it's much too small, of course."

Of course. Pat was beginning to understand, although she still had one more question. "Then if it's their house, why wouldn't they come in to look for the ball? The way they acted, I thought the house was haunted or something."

"That's Nat for you. You have to really know Nat." Barbara sighed. "It's his pride. My mother says the Paines were always proud. The day they moved out, he made the others take some kind of dopey vow that they wouldn't enter this house again until it was rightfully theirs. Just like in a book. You know how boys are."

Pat didn't know how boys are. But she had followed enough of Barbara's explanation to feel a spark of sympathy for the Paines, in spite of the way they had acted.

"Gosh, maybe we shouldn't be here either," she said.

"Oh pooh. That's silly. I come here lots of times." Barbara tossed her head. "It's a keen place to explore. I'm sure there's a secret passageway, if I just knew where to look. Want to help me find it sometime?"

"Sometime." Pat turned her head toward the garden. The boys were shouting. The sun was shining. And she still hadn't ridden her bike or climbed a tree. "Let's do it the next rainy day," she proposed.

5 | Making Friends

D<small>INNER IN THE</small> H<small>ARRISON HOUSEHOLD</small> that night was a silent affair. Mother and Dad were too tired to talk, and Pat was still trying to sort out the information that Barbara had given her.

"Did you have a good ball game?" Mother asked, as she put the dessert on the table. She sounded interested, but Pat suspected that she was really thinking about where to hang the spice shelf and the picture that Aunt Alice had sent.

"Uh huh." Pat nodded. "Made one terrific hit. Even the boys were surprised. But, Mother — Dad — what's 'lostitfortaxes'?"

Dad lifted his eyebrows. "When anyone in Haven says that, they're sure to be talking about the Paine house."

"What do you mean, Joe?" Mother asked.

"That old house next door. I *know* I told you about it," he replied. "After Nate Paine was killed, Betsy couldn't keep it up. The town council sort of overlooked it for several years, but finally they said she'd have to move. In a way she's better off. That house is a white elephant. Still has the furnace that Nate's great-grandfather installed during the Civil War, and the plumbing's probably older."

"It's such a perfect example of an old salt box," Mother said. "I've been wanting to walk over and have a look at it."

This was as confusing as listening to Barbara. How could a house be a white elephant and a salt box all at the same time? "Well, I think it's awful," Pat interrupted. "All three of them sleeping in one room and —"

"It certainly doesn't take you long to pick up the local gossip." Dad smiled. "I'm surprised that the boys told you about it. They were always a very close-mouthed family."

"Not the boys." Pat shook her head. "A girl came over. Barbara Thomas."

"That explains it then," Dad said. "The only person who can talk more than Dorothy Thomas is her husband, Dick. Their daughter must take after them. You remember the Thomases" — he turned to his wife — "next door to Mother?"

Mrs. Harrison nodded. "I'm awfully glad you've met a girl to play with. Would you like to invite her to lunch sometime, Pat?"

Pat gulped. "I . . . I — already did. Tomorrow. We'll fix our own lunch and clean up, though," she added, as she saw the expression on her mother's face.

"All right." Mrs. Harrison sighed. "But you must play outdoors. I still have lots of straightening out to do."

Pat smiled her thanks. While she was drying the dishes, she asked one of the questions which was puzzling her. "A salt box? What's a salt box?"

"A kind of house built in Colonial times," Mother explained. "It was called 'salt box,' I guess, because it was shaped like the boxes the colonists kept salt in. There were two stories and an attic in front usually, and a story and a half, or only one, in the rear." She stopped because she thought that Pat was losing interest.

"What about secret passageways? Did they put them in salt boxes?" Pat wanted to know.

"I doubt it." Her mother laughed. "The houses were very simple then. They didn't even have things like closets or bathrooms or furnaces. All the heat came from big fireplaces. If you're interested, maybe we can get permission from Mrs. Paine to visit the house next door and look around."

"I —" Pat was about to tell her mother that she had already visited the Paine house when Dad called from the living room. He wanted to know if Aunt Alice's picture was supposed to go over the couch or next to the window. By the time Mother decided about the picture and asked Dad what he thought about draperies for the dining room, Pat had finished with the dishes and was heading up the stairs.

The next morning Barbara appeared at the front door even before Mother took Dad to the station. Sitting Indian-style on the floor of Pat's room, she chattered away while Pat hung up her clothes and made her bed. She talked about the teachers in school and the girls and boys, until Pat was beginning to feel as if she had always lived in Haven.

When Pat was ready — and properly dressed today, in dungarees, striped T shirt, and a pair of worn red sneakers — they went out to the garage for their bikes. Mrs. Harrison was putting the car away.

"Where are you going, girls?" she asked.

"Downtown. I thought I'd show Pat the sights," Barbara answered.

Mrs. Harrison hesitated. "I'm delighted to have you show her around, of course, but I'm a little worried about the biking. Pat hasn't ever ridden in traffic before."

Pat was embarrassed, but before she could protest, Barbara was nodding wisely at Mrs. Harrison.

"I know just how you feel," she assured her. "My mother was the same way until I got to be a member of the Safety Patrol. Would you like me to recite 'Twenty Rules for Safe Bicycling'? Keep to the right. Ride single file. Know your hand signals. Stop at red lights —"

"Stop, stop." Mrs. Harrison held up her own hand. "I guess you know what you're doing. Have a good time, the two of you, and don't be late for lunch."

As they wheeled their bikes out of the driveway, Pat looked down at Barbara approvingly. "You know, you're very good with mothers," she said.

"I'm very good, period," the little girl announced. Tugging at her dungarees, she pretended to curtsy.

From the Harrison house they rode down the hill and around the corner, until they had biked along Old Post Road to downtown Haven. To celebrate her first trip on the road on a bike, Pat treated Barbara to a chocolate sundae with marshmallow and nuts and whipped cream, and a cherry on top. To celebrate her first time alone in Haven stores, she bought a banana split for herself, even though she didn't usually eat banana splits because they were fattening.

Back home, after finishing peanut-butter sandwiches and some cake that Grandma had brought, they decided to climb trees. Barbara's legs were short and Pat's were long, but Barbara could shinny right up the trunks, while Pat was still trying to lift her feet from the ground. With much huffing and puffing, Pat managed to climb the maple tree out front, but the oak at the side of the house, whose branches reached to her bedroom window, was too hard for her.

"City girl," Barbara teased as she sat on a limb of the oak tree, swinging her legs. "What you need is an elevator."

Pat didn't really mind Barbara's teasing, but when Jim came over and asked them to play, she was glad of a change. The Paines were waiting for them on the old stone wall at the back of her yard. For the rest of the afternoon, everyone chanted:

> I'm the king of the castle
> And you're the dirty rascal,

and ran and tumbled and laughed.

Now that Pat knew about the Paines, and wasn't playing baseball with them, they weren't so bad. Johnny was almost as nice as Jim, and although Sam was terribly tough for such a little boy, he was cute. He had been reading stories about King Arthur and the knights of the Round Table, and whenever he got excited he said "Gad, sir" instead of "Gee whiz" or "Gosh." Nat — well, she still didn't exactly like Nat, but she felt sort of sorry for him.

The next day and the day after were more of the same. There were long, sunny hours of bicycle riding and tree climbing and games. Pat learned to climb hand over hand to the top of the clump of birches in Jim's yard, and she could just about get up in the oak if someone stayed behind to give her a boost.

The nights promised to be as good as the days. Although it was still their first week in the new house, and they weren't what Mother called settled, Barbara was allowed to sleep in the extra bed in Pat's room.

"Then it'll be your turn to sleep at my house," Barbara pointed out as they were getting undressed.

Pat nodded happily. Things were working out even better than she had expected. After she had buttoned her pajamas, she pulled back the curtain to look out of the window, to see the yard and the trees and the fields and the houses of Haven. Somewhere nearby a bird was whistling.

"Listen!" She was excited. "Do you suppose that's an owl? I never heard an owl before."

Barbara groaned. "An owl! Gosh, can't you tell the difference between an owl and a whippoorwill, silly? Don't you hear it saying 'whip-poor-will, whip-poor-will'?"

Pat flattened her nose against the screen, to see if she could spot the bird. The night was dark, but way off beyond the stone wall she thought she saw something move. Way off in the shadows of the deserted garden.

"Look!" She grabbed Barbara's arm.

Way off, past the wall, past the orchard, past the garden, there was a light. A light was bobbing up and down in the old Paine house!

6 | The Man in the Kitchen

PAT FELT AROUND FOR BARBARA'S HAND. "There's no such thing as ghosts," she loudly announced.

"Who said anything about ghosts?" Barbara snorted. "Someone's got a flashlight. We'd better go over and see what he's up to."

He? We? "What makes you think he's up to anything?" Pat asked. "Maybe he just went in to look around."

"In the middle of the night?" Barbara snorted again. "He's looking for the secret passageway where the treasure is hidden."

"What secret passage? What treasure?"

"Well, I don't exactly know for sure." Barbara kept her eyes on the window and talked out of the side of her mouth. "But lots of people in Haven think there must be one. Because long ago the family was rich. Clipper ships and all that sort of stuff. Then the father and mother were killed in the Revolution, and when their children came back there wasn't any money or anything."

"But Barbara, that was hundreds of years ago," Pat protested. "Someone would have been sure to find any treasure before now."

"But they didn't," Barbara pointed out. "Besides — Look, he's going into the kitchen. We'd better hurry." She unhooked the window screen and began to push it out.

Pat stared. "Where do you think you're going?"

"Out the window. To spy on him. See what he's doing, of course."

Of course. Naturally. Sometimes it was hard being a country girl. Pat swallowed. "But my parents . . . Let's tell them, and then my father —"

"Your parents are at your grandmother's," Barbara reminded her. "Remember, they said they'd be back in an hour, and did we think we'd be all right. Come on now. Hurry!" She lifted up the screen and swung a pajama-covered leg over the window sill.

"B-b-but why the window?" Pat stuttered.

"Quickest way," the little girl assured her. "Look,

here's this big limb of the oak tree. Just grab it and sort of slide along till you get to the trunk. After that you can jump. I noticed how simple it was when I was boosting you up this afternoon. I was going to suggest that we try it then, only the boys came over."

"Simple for you, maybe," Pat argued. "Not so simple for me."

"Look." Straddling the window sill, Barbara pointed in the direction of the old Paine house. "Do you want to let *him* get away with it? Do you want *him* to steal the treasure that rightfully belongs to the Paines? Do you want them to lose their house, when we could save it for them?"

There was something wrong with Barbara's argument, but Pat didn't have time to figure it out. Barbara wasn't waiting to hear the answers to her questions. She was outside the window already, sliding across the broad limb of oak and whispering, "C'mon."

Barefooted, in her pajamas, Pat came. There was nothing else for her to do. After all, if Barbara, who was a whole head shorter than she, was going to climb out of the window and down the tree, well, she couldn't let her go alone.

Sitting astride the oak limb, she humped herself over until she reached the trunk. Then she looked down at Barbara, who was waiting impatiently for her at the foot of the tree. It was a *long* way down to the ground. Closing her eyes, holding her breath, she half slid, half jumped.

"Neat," Barbara whispered approvingly, as Pat picked herself up.

Pat looked longingly at the curtained living-room window. But it would be another half-hour, any-way, before her parents returned, and by then —

"Hurry," Barbara urged.

The two girls hurried. They stubbed their toes on the wobbly stone wall, and they caught their pa-jamas on brambles as they crossed the field. They stumbled in the orchard, and they tripped in the garden, and they tiptoed to the kitchen window of the old Paine house.

Even Barbara was breathless as they looked in-side. There really was a man in the kitchen! Not an ordinary-looking man either, like their fathers or the teachers in school, but a man with a curly black beard which covered half his face!

Holding a flashlight in front of him as if it were a gun, he studied the room. Something about the

47

fireplace seemed particularly interesting to him. With his free hand, he reached inside an opening in the fireplace wall and lifted out a brick.

"What'd I tell you?" Barbara's lips framed the words that she didn't dare to say out loud.

Pat nodded an answer, and Barbara nudged her to complete the conversation. The nudge proved fatal. Pat swayed. Pat tottered. One moment, she was squatting on her heels, with her chin on the kitchen window sill. The next, she was lying on her back in a tangle of roses and thorns.

The man with the flashlight stood stock-still. The bearded man with the flashlight in his hand, and goodness-only-knew-what in his pocket, looked toward the noise. Before he could flash his light at her, Barbara ducked.

She meant to hide below the window ledge so that the man couldn't see her. But she hadn't counted on the thorny branches of the rosebush, or on Pat's waving arms and flailing legs. She hadn't counted on toppling over into the bush where Pat was lying.

Before the girls could disentangle themselves, they heard footsteps in the kitchen. They heard footsteps in the hall. They clutched each other's hands, as the footsteps passed the front door, paused, and then clattered down the path that led to New Street.

The bearded man wasn't looking for them. He was running away from the old Paine house just as fast as he could run!

7 | Pre-posterous!

PAT AND BARBARA RAN TOO. They raced through the garden and across the field and over the wall to the Harrisons'. Then they ran up the stairs and breathlessly flung themselves on the beds in Pat's room. They felt as if they had been away for hours, but it was only fifteen minutes by the clock since they had opened the window and slid down the oak tree.

"Thank goodness Mother and Dad'll be home soon," Pat said when she had caught her breath. "We can wait up and tell them."

Barbara thought about this for a moment, then shook her head. "They'll go into orbit about it, won't they? At least my parents would. They'll call the police and my mother, and they won't let me stay overnight any more and all that stuff."

51

Pat sighed. The idea of a policeman who would look for the bearded man was wonderfully comforting. But the possibility of Barbara being sent home and not allowed to come over any more — She sighed again. Life was more complicated in Haven than in New York.

"Well, suppose I tell Mother in the morning," she compromised. "I mean, it won't sound so . . . so scary then, and she probably won't do anything about it. Or not much, anyway."

"Okay." Barbara still sounded doubtful, but if that was the way Pat wanted it, it was all right with her.

Only Pat didn't tell her mother in the morning. It was after nine when the girls awakened, and there was a note on the kitchen table when they went downstairs.

"Broke my glasses at Grandma's," the note explained. "I'm going to have new ones made soon as I take Dad to the station. There's orange juice in the jar and bananas for your cereal. Love, Mother."

Barbara poured the orange juice and milk, while Pat sliced bananas. They were spooning sugar on their cereal when Jim appeared at the door.

"Baseball, anybody?" he asked.

"Not today," Barbara loftily announced. "We have more important matters to attend to."

Ordinarily, Jim didn't believe that there could be anything more important than baseball. But when he had listened to the girls' story of the night before, he forgot all about the game.

A telephone call soon brought the Paines to the Harrisons' kitchen. Johnny's eyes grew bright, and Sam murmured, "Gad, sir!" over and over again, as Barbara told them about the bearded man.

Only Nat refused to become excited. "Pre-posterous," he growled. "You're the biggest storyteller in the whole town, Barbara Thomas. Everyone in Haven knows that."

"Am *not!*" For a moment, it seemed as if Barbara was going to get into an argument with Nat. Then she thought better of it. "It's true, every word of it. Cross my heart. Scout's honor."

"It's really, truly true." Pat backed her up. "Besides, if you don't believe it, we can go over to the house and see. I bet the brick he took out of the fireplace is still lying on the floor."

"Let's go!" Jim slid off the kitchen stool. "What are we waiting for?"

Nat frowned. Nat glowered at his brothers. "Our vow," he reminded them. "You promised never to set foot in the house until —"

"But this is an emergency," Johnny argued.

"An emergency," Sam echoed.

"Like if somebody was drowning," Jim backed them up. "If a person was drowning, you'd come to their rescue, wouldn't you?"

Nat's only reply was a grunt. After thinking it over for a moment, he turned on his heel and headed for the door. The others followed.

When they drew near the open kitchen window of the old house, Nat shook his head. Steering them around to the front, he pulled open the heavy oak door and motioned them inside.

"No need for us to be sneaking in the window," he scolded. "It isn't as if we don't have any right to go in."

Pat felt a flash of sympathy as she looked up into his scowling face. When he stood there holding the door open, he was sort of like a king, inviting people to enter his castle. Except that it wasn't going to be his castle much longer. Maybe if she had lost her father and was losing her home too, maybe she'd be all mean and proud the way he was.

The next minute she forgot about Nat. Because, as soon as her eyes grew accustomed to the dim light, she could see the brick lying on the hearth, exactly where the bearded man had been standing. And next to the brick, there was a battered black flashlight.

"Cool!"

"Keen-o!"

"Gad, sir!"

Everyone whistled and scrambled for the flashlight. There was nothing remarkable about it. It was only the two-battery kind, with a ring on the end so that you could hang it on a hook or fasten it to your belt if you were hiking. But it was passed from hand to hand, until each boy and girl had seen it and felt it and switched it on and switched it off. It was passed from hand to hand until Nat said "fingerprints" in such a pained tone that Sam dropped the flashlight on the floor. It rolled across the worn wooden floor boards, coming to rest beneath the window.

"That's no way to handle a flashlight," a booming voice complained. "You've probably broken it."

A man was standing outside and leaning on the window sill. Not an ordinary-looking man, like their fathers or the teachers in school, but a man with a curly black beard which covered half of his face! He stretched out his arm toward the flashlight. His fingers were touching the dull metal, when Nat grabbed his arm.

"Hey," the bearded man protested. "What do you think you're doing?"

Instead of answering, Nat caught his brothers'

eyes and jerked his head in the direction of the front door. While they ran outside, Jim reached for the man's other arm. Soon Johnny had hold of one leg and Sam another, and the bearded man was leaning across the window sill, unable to move.

"Cut it out," their prisoner ordered. "What kind of crazy game is this? You're making me feel like a seesaw."

"Never mind how you feel." Nat was using his gruffest voice. "You're the one who has explaining to do. Talk!"

8 | Mr. Popham Talks

"LISTEN, YOU BUNCH OF JUVENILE DELINQUENTS, I'll talk plenty," the man bellowed. "To the police and to your parents. It's fine for you to play cowboys and bad men. Good clean fun and all that. But when you attack an innocent bystander —"

"The police!" Jim snorted.

"Innocent!" Barbara mocked.

"Robber!" Johnny accused.

"I suppose you didn't break in last night?" Pat demanded to know. "I suppose this isn't your flashlight?" She held it up by the ring.

"Last night?" the man repeated in a puzzled voice. "Where were you kids last night?"

Six pairs of eyes stared at him, but six mouths

57

clamped closed. A strange expression came over the man's face. Because of the beard it was hard to tell, but it looked — it certainly did seem — as if his anger was disappearing and embarrassment was taking its place.

"Don't tell me that racket outside . . . ? Don't tell me that all that noise was you," he pleaded.

"Not all of us," Barbara modestly explained. "Just Pat and me."

He turned his head to see who had spoken, then groaned. "Four feet nine in her socks — seventy pounds dripping wet after a big meal — and I ran. . . .

"Kids." He straightened up so abruptly that everyone let go of him. Then he swung his legs over the sill and into the kitchen. "I want you to promise never to tell a single soul."

"We're not making any promises to you. Talk," Nat sternly ordered. "What were you up to, here?"

The man laughed. "You'll never believe it. Nobody ever will," he informed them. "But I was carrying on research. Historical research. Rise of American civilization and such."

Historical research? American civilization? Jim looked at Nat, and Nat frowned at Pat, but no one wanted to admit that he didn't understand. Only

Barbara had the glimmering of an idea. Looking up, she thoughtfully studied the stranger's face.

"He's not really a man," she announced.

"Not a man?" Pat was puzzled.

"In disguise?" Jim asked.

"Fake beard?" Sam reached out and gave it a tug.

"Ouch," their captive complained. He waved his arms and pushed Sam away. "Leave my beard alone."

"He's not really a man," Barbara explained. "He's a college boy. When David — that's my brother — came home from college last Christmas, he had a beard too, and he talked like that, with all sorts of big words. Daddy told Mother not to pay any attention to it, that it was just a stage boys go through, like joining the Scouts or falling in love."

The stranger moaned.

"Are you a college boy?" Nat asked.

The stranger groaned. "Don't they teach children respect for their elders any more? Sure I go to college. To York University on the outskirts of Haven. But if I'd known that there were monsters like you living here, I'd have picked the University of California instead."

"What'd I tell you?" Barbara smiled in triumph.

Nat thought the matter over. Even if he *was* a college boy, he still had plenty to explain. "What were you doing here?" he demanded to know.

The bearded college-boy-man made himself comfortable on the window sill, and the boys and girls sank to the floor, waiting. "Not that it's any concern of yours," the stranger informed his wary audience, "but my name's Robert Popham — *Mr.* Popham to you. And I'm writing a history paper."

"What about?" Jim asked.

"American Revolution around Haven. Battles and —"

"There weren't any big battles here." Nat challenged him. "The British held New York and the Americans were across the river, and they called this 'the neutral ground.'"

"Smart boy." Mr. Popham looked surprised. "How'd you know that? My paper's mostly on the local people. How they lived during the war, which ones were for the rebels, and which ones were the Tories who sympathized with the British."

"How come you're writing it now?" Barbara was still suspicious. "It's vacation. York closed weeks ago."

"Smart girl." Mr. Popham smiled. He had a pretty nice smile if you looked behind the beard.

"I was sick this winter, so my professor said I could stay on and finish the paper now. Last night I was reading in the college library. They've got a whole stack of old papers and letters in the basement that nobody's ever been through. Stuff people gave them that they haven't had the money to catalogue."

Sam stirred restlessly, and Johnny slumped back on the floor. It was disappointing enough to have their bearded villain turn out to be a college boy, but if he was only going to talk about libraries and old letters —

"I was reading a letter from Nathaniel Woodruff when I suddenly realized that this must be the old Woodruff house."

Woodruff? Pat started to tell him that he was wrong, but the others motioned to her to be quiet.

"Of course I'd seen the house every time I drove by on Old Post Road, but I never connected it with the Woodruff family before," Mr. Popham continued. "They're one of the families I'm covering in my paper. So after the library closed, I came over to look at it. The house, I mean. It seemed empty, and the front door wasn't locked, so I walked in."

"The flashlight? What were you doing with the flashlight?" Jim wanted to know.

Mr. Popham shook his head in despair. "I took it

from the glove compartment of my car. What would *you* do with a flashlight if you were walking through a dark house at night?" When no one answered, he continued to talk. "You know, this is an interesting old place. The man who originally owned it was probably the leading Tory in Haven during the Revolution. In my paper —"

"Tory!" Sam's eyes flashed.

"Tory!" Johnny yelled.

"Tory! You take that back!" Nat doubled up his fists and moved threateningly toward Mr. Popham.

9 | Nathaniel Woodruff's Letter

"HEY, STOP!" Jim grabbed Nat's arm and tried to calm him down.

"Are you crazy?" Mr. Popham wanted to know. "I don't want to hurt you, but if you take a poke at me I'm liable to forget that you're only a little kid."

Nat's face was pale and his eyes black as coal. "You take it back," he shouted.

"Take what back? That you're only a little kid?" The stranger unfolded his legs and stood up. He was almost a head taller than Nat.

"Not that," Nat growled. "What you said before. About Nathaniel Woodruff being a Tory."

Mr. Popham stroked his beard thoughtfully. "I'm not interested in fighting the Revolution all over again. I'll take it back if you'll give me a good reason why I should."

"Because — because —" Nat spluttered. "Well, because my name is Nathaniel Woodruff Paine the Fourth. Because the first Nathaniel Woodruff who built this house way my great-great- —"

"Great- —" Johnny added.

"Great- —" Sam echoed.

"Great-great-grandfather."

So *that* was it! Pat suddenly understood. Nat had gotten mad because he didn't like to hear that his great-grandfather had been on the British side in the Revolution.

"You're really a Woodruff descendant?" Mr. Popham beamed. "That's terrific. I had no idea there were any still living in Haven."

"The three of us." Taken off guard for a moment, Nat sounded almost friendly, as he pointed to his brothers.

"Pleased to meet you." The student stooped over to shake each Paine boy's hand. "And you?" He turned inquiringly to the others.

"Only friends of the family," Barbara explained. "This is Patricia Harrison and Jim Gray. And I'm Barbara Thomas."

"Glad to meet you too. Any friends of the Woodruffs are friends of mine," Mr. Popham announced, as he sat down on the hearthstone in front of the fireplace. "Just call me Robert," he added.

Pat giggled. He was turning out to be nice, in spite of the beard.

Only Nat refused to be won over. "Take it back," he repeated.

"You may be right." Robert slowly shook his head. "But most of the evidence is against you. Articles in the old papers, people's letters, they all say he was a Tory. Even his own correspondence shows that he went back and forth to New York during the British occupation. Come over to the library with me, and I'll show you a pass made out for Nathaniel Woodruff and signed by General Henry Clinton."

Nat scowled. Johnny whistled softly. Sam groaned.

"Who's Henry Clinton?" Pat whispered.

"British general," Barbara whispered back. "Sort of boss of New York during the Revolution. Until we chased him out."

Pat sighed. Things certainly looked bad for Great-grandpa Woodruff.

"No need to feel upset about it," Robert continued. "Lots of people were Tories in those days.

I bet you've been to Philipse Castle over in Tarry-town, haven't you?"

Everyone but Pat nodded. It was a favorite field trip for Haven history classes.

"Well, the Philipse family were Tories during the Revolution. They ran off to England, and the Americans confiscated their property. Didn't your history teacher tell you that?"

"We're not talking about the Philipses." Nat refused to be consoled. "The Woodruff's weren't Tories. Why, George Washington even slept here," he argued. "Right in the front bedroom upstairs."

"But that was at the beginning of the war," Johnny reminded him. "Maybe later —"

Nat glared at his brother. "And Lafayette too," he continued.

"That was way later," Sam pointed out. "I forget when, but long after the Revolution was over."

"Eighteen twenty-four," Nat gloomily admitted. His chin sank to his chest, and he began to nibble at a fingernail.

"There's one possibility." Robert was trying to cheer him up now. "It occurred to me last night when I was reading at the library. Of course I can't prove it, but — Everyone around here thought that Nathaniel Woodruff was a Tory, but it just may be that he was a spy."

A spy? Pat watched Nat to see what he would say. She wasn't sure if he was going to get angry all over again. Was it good or bad to be a spy?

"Do you mean —" Jim thought out loud. "Like Nathan Hale — 'I have only one life to give for my country'?"

"Like Nathan Hale." Robert nodded. "Only Hale got caught on his very first spying trip. And if I'm right about Woodruff, he must have been a spy for a good part of the war."

Nat stopped chewing his nails. He raised his head and snapped his fingers instead. "Why didn't I think of that? Remember in front of the Bible" — he turned to his brothers — "where it says when everybody died and where and all? For Nathaniel Woodruff, it just says 'Died, 1781.' No month, no day, no nothing. Bet that was 'cause the British caught him and shot him."

"Hanged him," Robert gently suggested. "At least that's what they did with Nathan Hale."

"And we did to Major André," Barbara remembered.

Pat turned her head from one to the other, as if she were watching a tennis game. They seemed to know so much more history than she did. Maybe it was catching, and now that she lived next to a historic old house she'd learn some too.

"Are you sure he died in 1781?" Robert asked Nat. "That's the same year he wrote the letter I found in the library."

Nat nodded. He was sure.

"It was that letter, really, that made me want to come here and look around," Robert continued. "Something so human about it that, well, I guess he didn't sound like my idea of a Tory either."

"What'd he write?"

"Who'd he write to?"

"To his wife, Deborah. Wait, I copied some of it down." Robert reached into his breast pocket for a notebook. "He starts off saying, 'Leaving this day for New York on a journey from which there may be no return.' Then he says he's troubled about what will become of her and their infant son, Nathaniel, if he dies."

"See," Nat interrupted. "He *must* have been a spy. Else why would he expect to die on a trip to New York?"

"After all, my father goes there every day." Jim tried a joke.

" 'Having neither musket nor uniform' " — Robert continued to read from his notebook — " 'I desire him to have the book and such other treasures as are in the old postbox.' "

"Treasures!" Johnny's eyes gleamed.

"Gad, sir!" Sam took a deep breath, and Barbara poked an elbow into Pat's side.

Robert frowned, as if he didn't like being interrupted. " 'You will know where to look for these, taking care not to burn your hands as you secure them. Only when this terrible war is over can he learn the truth about his father.' The rest is about entrusting the letter to a friend to deliver, and asking Deborah to convey his greetings to 'madam, your mother.' I figured Deborah was off with the baby, visiting her mother, when he wrote."

"Cool!"

"Keen, man!"

It took a minute before Nat could make himself heard. "It figures," he triumphantly announced. "Having no musket or uniform, and telling his son the truth after the war. 'Course he was a spy."

"And the treasure —"

"The postbox —"

Jumping up, Sam headed for the front door. He was in the hall when Johnny called, "Where do you think you're going?"

"The postbox — that old mailbox at the end of the path — I thought —" He turned back as everyone groaned. "I know we've looked in it a million times,

70

but it might have a false bottom or something. Haven't you ever read about false bottoms?" He tried to defend himself.

"Your head's got a false bottom," Johnny informed him. "How old do you suppose that mailbox is? They didn't even have mailboxes in 1781."

Sam slumped to the floor, poking out his underlip in a pout. That was the trouble with older brothers. They always acted as if they knew everything. He picked up the brick which was lying on the hearth and began to play with it.

" 'Taking care not to burn your hands.' " Pat repeated the phrase from the letter. "What do you suppose he meant by that?"

Nat stared at a crack in the floor, thinking.

"It's a clue," Jim announced.

"Of course it's a clue," Barbara agreed. "He was telling her where the postbox was hidden —"

"Where the *treasure* was hidden," Johnny interrupted.

"Where could you burn your hands? A stove?" Pat suggested.

"Not a stove." Barbara bounced up and down. "Because they didn't have stoves in the olden days. They cooked in their fireplaces!"

Everyone turned to gape at the big brick fireplace across the room. Everyone except Nat. He reached for the brick that Sam had been balancing on his knee and waved it at Robert.

"That's what you were doing here last night. You were looking for the treasure. You were going to steal our treasure!"

"Wait!" the college boy counseled him. "Not so fast. In the first place, old Nathaniel never hid the kind of treasure you're thinking about. 'The book and other treasures' — he was talking of papers, not diamonds or pieces of eight."

"Then what were you poking around the fireplace for? They" — Nat jerked his head in Pat and Barbara's direction — "saw you take out this brick."

Robert moaned softly and shook his head. "Look, I'm a history student. I was interested in old Woodruff's letter, sure. And being just as smart as you kids, I figured that he'd hidden his box somewhere around a fireplace. Couldn't have been under the hearth, because the stone's too heavy for his wife to have lifted. Maybe it was in the bake oven. When I put my hand in there, I felt a loose brick and took it out. But I didn't take out any treasure and I didn't expect to find one. Because whatever it was that Nathaniel hid, Deborah found it about one hundred and eighty years ago."

"How do you know?" Nat was still suspicious.

"Be reasonable, man," Robert answered. "He wrote her that he was hiding something. 'You'll know where to look for it,' he said. Why ever wouldn't she find it?"

Instead of answering, Nat asked a question of his own. "What was the date on Nathaniel Woodruff's letter?"

Robert consulted his notebook. "April 19, 1781."

"Then you're wrong," Nat crowed.

"Wrong?"

"Great-grandma Deborah never found the treasure. It must be still here."

"How can you say that?" Pat edged into the debate.

"Because" — Nat tapped the floor with the brick to emphasize his words — "Deborah — Woodruff — died — on — the — eighteenth — of — April, 1781. The day before the letter was ever written!"

10 Behind the Bricks

Everyone was suddenly shouting at once. Pat's head was spinning. First Great-grandpa Woodruff was a Tory. Then he wasn't a Tory but an American spy. He hid a treasure which Great-grandma should have found. Only she didn't find it because she was dead.

"You can't be sure of the date," Robert argued.

"Can too!" Nat was always sure of everything. "I remembered that date because it's the same day as Paul Revere's ride, only a different year."

"'On the eighteenth of April in seventy-five, hardly a man is now alive,'" Pat started to recite. She didn't know much history, but once she had recited all fifteen verses of "Paul Revere's Ride" in a school assembly.

"Shush." Barbara nudged her again.

"Besides," Nat continued, "I particularly remember about Great-grandma Deborah, because whoever wrote about her in our Bible said that she was 'foully murdered.' "

"That's right," Johnny agreed. "We used to think it was the Indians. That they scalped her. But now do you suppose it was the British?"

"You mean the British scalped Great-grandma Deborah?" Sam asked, tugging at the lock of hair that was hanging in his eyes.

"Not scalped — just killed, stupid," his brother informed him.

"More likely she was killed by the cowboys," Robert suggested.

Cowboys? The boys and girls turned on him in disgust. This was no time for making jokes. Even college boys with beards ought to know that cowboys didn't go around killing people. They were lawmen, not outlaws.

"How could it have been cowboys?" Jim asked. "For one thing, they live out west, not in Haven."

Robert was gleeful. "At last I've found something that I know and you kids don't. The very first cowboys in the whole country lived in New

York State during the Revolution. They were British sympathizers, and they traveled around in bands, stealing and murdering. I've got a whole section in my paper on the cowboys in Haven."

"Why'd they call them that?" Pat wanted to know.

"Because they specialized in stealing cows. Which they then drove to New York and sold to the British."

A bumblebee flew in the window and buzzed overhead. The children watched its heavy-bodied flight as they digested Robert's information. It was interesting, if true, but not half as exciting as the possibility of finding honest-to-goodness secret, hidden treasure.

Abruptly, Nat stood up. Walking across the room, he picked up Robert's flashlight and shone it on the waist-high square opening in the fireplace wall. Then he reached inside and pulled out a brick.

"Funny, I never noticed before. Lots of the bricks in the bake oven are loose," he commented.

"Bake oven?" This time Pat poked her elbow into Barbara's ribs.

"Where they used to cook, stupe," Barbara explained. "They lit a fire in there, and the bricks got all hot, and they baked bread or roasted meat and stuff."

Pat stood up so that she could look into the oven. It was much bigger than her mother's. "But I thought they cooked over the fire." She pointed to the iron cranes that were fastened to the inside of the fireplace. "With pots hanging from those hooks. That's the way they had it arranged in the museum."

"That was for boiling things, like soups or stews," Robert added.

Nat cleared his throat noisily. "Maybe when the cooking lesson is over, we can get down to business. These loose bricks —" He removed another one and laid it on the hearth. "The treasure —"

Robert shook his head. "Of course the bricks are loose. Originally they were cemented together with clay, not the mortar that people use now. While the Woodruff ladies were cooking here, the heat from their fires hardened the clay. Now that the fireplace isn't being used, the clay has dried out. No mystery about that. You're not going to find any treasure."

"But if Deborah was killed —"

"And she never got the letter —"

"And their child was only a baby —"

"Well then," Pat summed up for everyone, "the treasure must still be here. If we only knew where it was."

"How many people do you suppose have lived in this house since 1781?" Robert asked. "What happened to Nathaniel, Jr., for instance?"

"Came back here when he was a young man. Married Abigail Something-or-other," Nat promptly replied. "They had seven daughters, no sons. Lucy — she was the oldest daughter — she married Isaac Paine and they got to keep the house. After that, there was Jonathan Paine, and then —"

"Exactly what I mean," Robert interrupted. "All those people. Don't you suppose one of those seven daughters would have found the postbox if it was in the bake oven?"

Secretly, Pat agreed with him. If *she'd* been a girl living in this house, *she* would have found the treasure.

"Impossible," Nat argued. "Or I'd know about it. We've got trunks full of stuff about the Woodruff's and the Paines — letters, diaries, pictures — and there's not one single word about a treasure."

"Trunks full?" Robert's eyes lit up. "Material about old Nathaniel? Could I see it?"

"That's what I'm trying to tell you." Nat was impatient. "There's nothing about the first Nathaniel, except that he built this house. And the dates in the Bible. Born 1755, died 1781. If his son or granddaughters or anybody found his treasure, there'd be —"

"Seventeen fifty-five to seventeen eighty-one. He lived to be only twenty-six," Barbara sighed. "How sad."

Nat frowned at the interruption. "You all talk too much. I'm going to work." He turned his back on them and reached into the bake oven again.

Johnny and Jim joined him. Sam tried to too, but the older boys elbowed him out of the way. Pretty soon there were half a dozen bricks lying on the hearth.

After watching them for a few minutes, Robert shook his head. "You stop right this minute, or I'm going to call your father," he scolded. "Even if this is your house, you have no right to destroy it. Even if you don't care about it, other people do. It's one of the last eighteenth-century houses around here."

"Even if — even if — " Nat looked as if he was about to throw the brick in his hand at Robert. "Since you know so much, you ought to know that this isn't our house any more. Or it won't be on August fifteenth, when it's going to be sold by the town of Haven. Unless — unless we can find the Woodruff treasure and pay the taxes we owe." He turned back to the oven again. His voice was muffled as he finished. "And you can't call my father because he's dead."

Robert's cheeks were red above the beard, and he swallowed hard. "Sorry, fellow," he said in a gentler voice. "I didn't know how much the chance of finding this treasure meant to you. I thought it was sort of a game."

"Okay," Nat gruffly replied. "Forget it."

"Maybe," Robert said, "I could give you a couple of suggestions before I leave. Maybe — "

"Leave?" Pat asked.

"Where you going?" Barbara wanted to know.

"You just came," Sam complained.

"After that friendly welcome you gave me, I should have known you'd want me to stick around." Robert laughed. "Unfortunately I just happen to have a paper to write, and I'm driving home — back to Ohio — in the morning, so I can finish it there."

"Gosh," Johnny said, "we could use you. I mean, you know about the Woodruffs and all. Maybe you could help us find the treasure."

"Wish I could stick around to help." Robert looked as if he meant it. "I was thinking last night about Nathaniel Woodruff's letter. If he was a spy, he probably put his messages in a regular hiding place. Then someone else came along and picked them up to take to Washington."

"A confederate." Jim hissed the word.

Nat didn't move from the bake oven, but Pat could tell from the way he stiffened that he was listening.

"The postbox — that probably was what he called the box that he hid his messages in," Robert continued. "I figure it really was a box, tin most likely, and about the size of a toolbox." He gestured with his hands to show how big the box would have been. "At least that was the kind of thing people used to store their valuables."

"I saw one in the museum that was like that," Pat agreed. "But why did he tell Deborah to be careful not to burn her hands? Wouldn't she have known where he kept his tin box"

"It's my guess," Robert answered, "that he had a couple of different boxes and different hiding places, and he was telling Deborah which one she should look in for the 'treasures' he was leaving for their son."

"But" — Barbara was doing some thinking too — "if he had regular places where his confederates picked up his spy messages, they'd have to be pretty easy to find, wouldn't they? I mean, they couldn't take a whole fireplace apart every time they wanted a message."

"Exactly." Robert nodded. "*If* Nathaniel was a spy, and *if* his postbox was hidden around his fireplace, there must have been a hollow space for it, say behind one row of bricks. And you'd just have to take out a couple of bricks to find the box."

"*If* you knew where to look." Nat backed out of the oven to join the conversation.

"Yes and no. Even if you're just guessing," Robert argued, "you don't have to tear the walls down. You can lift out a brick here and there, looking for that hollow space."

The kitchen was quiet for a moment, as everyone tried to picture the tin box and the hollow space somewhere behind a row of bricks.

"And see here," Robert smiled. "I'm not saying there ever was a treasure, and I'm not saying you'll find it after all these years. But I sure wish you lots of luck. First week in August I'll be back to see how you made out."

"Thanks," Nat murmured, in the politest voice Pat had ever heard him use. "Thanks," he repeated, as he crossed the room and shook Robert's hand.

11 | If I Were Nathaniel Woodruff

"Meeting tomorrow, right after breakfast. Bring a flashlight . . . Meeting tomorrow after breakfast . . . bring a flashlight . . . Meeting . . . after breakfast . . . flashlight." Nat telephoned Jim. Jim telephoned Pat. Pat telephoned Barbara.

The grass was still wet with dew when Pat walked through the deserted garden to the old house. She was beginning to get used to playing with boys. They really weren't much different from girls, except that they were noisier and less polite. If you didn't let your feelings get hurt when they yelled "Dope" or "Oh crumb," or if you behaved like Barbara and answered them right back, you got along fine. At least with Jim and Johnny and Sam. Nat — well, Nat still was awfully bossy.

Take this meeting now. At other meetings Pat had attended, people elected a chairman and a secretary, and took turns saying what they thought should be done. But here, Nat was chairman and secretary all rolled into one, without any election, and he didn't give anybody else a chance to say a word.

"Battle stations," he announced as soon as everyone was assembled in the kitchen. "Sam, you're smallest, so I'm going to boost you into the bake oven to work on the bricks way at the back. Johnny, you take the woodbin underneath. Pat and Barbara, you're inside the fireplace. The fireplace wall — Jim and me. And remember, we're just taking out a brick here and there, looking for a hollow space, like Robert said."

"A hollow space and a tin box," Johnny chanted.

"A treasure!" Sam said.

Barbara opened her mouth to argue about the assignments, but before she could say a word Nat dumped the contents of a paper bag on the floor. He'd thought of everything — extra flashlights, battered table knives, a ruler, and a big ball of string. Even though he was bossy he did have good ideas.

Everyone did exactly what Nat said they should. Sam was on his hands and knees in the bake oven, shining his flashlight on the rear wall of brick.

Johnny crawled into the woodbin beneath him.
Jim and Nat worked on the broad expanse of wall.
Inside the fireplace, behind the black iron cranes
where pots used to hang, Pat and Barbara sat on
the floor and looked for loose bricks.

Everyone did exactly what Nat said — for a
while. Then Barbara, who could never sit still for
very long, decided to explore. Wriggling past Pat,
she carefully raised herself, until she was stand-

ing up straight, with her head and shoulders in
the chimney flue.

"Hey," she called. "It's neat in here. You ought
to see."

Her words were muffled by the thick brick wall,
and no one was quite sure what she was saying.
See what? Had she found something?

Sam sat up and bumped his head. Johnny
turned and scraped his knee. Nat and Jim dropped

their knives and tried to squeeze into the fireplace alongside Pat.

Pretty soon they were yelling "Oh shoot" and "Ouch" and "Watch out." They were yelling and bumping into each other and stepping on Pat's hands and feet. They pushed and shoved and tried to squeeze into the fireplace until Pat could hardly breathe. It was like the subway in New York during rush hour. Putting her hands out in front of her, she began to yell and shove too.

"Getting out," she shouted as she'd heard people shout in the subway. "Getting out," she called again.

To her surprise it worked. Johnny backed out. Jim backed out. Nat backed out. Pat crawled past them to sit on the kitchen floor and catch her breath.

At last Barbara bent her knees and lowered her head. Her face was streaked with soot and her hair veiled in spider webs. "It's neat in there," she happily reported. "You can see all the way up to the sky."

"The sky?"

"The sky? Is that all you saw?"

The boys were disgusted. Was that what the fuss was all about?

"But it's real interesting." Barbara tried to explain. "It goes all the way up to the roof. It's like, well, it made me think of Santa Claus."

Santa Claus, at a time like this! Nat rolled over onto the hearth and groaned. When he sat up, he had only one word for Barbara: "Girls!"

Barbara's pleased smile faded away. The way Nat said it, "girls" was a fighting word — and she was always ready for battle.

"See here, Nat Paine," she scolded. "You're not as smart as you think. There are about a million bricks in this fireplace-chimney-thingamajig. What's your mother going to say if she finds out you're taking the fireplace apart? Your whole treasure-hunting plan is just plain dumb."

"My mother doesn't have to find out," Nat loftily announced. "She knows already. And she thinks my plan is fine."

"Um-m-m." Johnny's eyebrows lifted and he cleared his throat as if he had something to say on the subject.

Nat frowned at his brother. "At least she came over with us last night, and we showed her how the bricks were loose and you could just lift them out. She said it was all right, if we made sure to put them back again."

"But did she really say your plan was fine?" Barbara persisted.

"Well." Nat looked uncomfortable. "You know how grownups are. I guess they don't really believe that people ever find hidden treasure. But she did say it was okay to try."

"She said" — Sam imitated his mother's voice — "that she guessed it was our only chance of saving the house."

"Only she doesn't think we have much of a chance," Johnny added with a sigh.

Barbara chewed on her lower lip. "I keep forgetting," she apologized. "I mean, it's like a game, only —"

"Only it's for real," Nat scowled. "For us, anyway."

Barbara nodded in agreement. Then her face brightened. "But you're still going about it the wrong way. The first thing to do is think."

"About what?" Johnny challenged her.

"About where the treasure's hidden. About where you would hide it if you were Nathaniel Woodruff."

The room was quiet, as the boys and Pat thought about what Barbara had said: "Where would you hide a treasure if you were Nathaniel Woodruff?"

"I'll tell you where I *wouldn't* hide it," Barbara announced. "Not in the bake oven, because he needed that for cooking. Or at least Deborah did."

90

The boys and Pat nodded slowly. Certainly their mothers would never allow a treasure to be hidden in the oven. Not even in wartime, or if their husbands were spies.

Thinking about her mother made Pat remember something she had said. "They used their fireplaces for heating too, so he wouldn't have hidden it in the part where you light the fire, where Barbara and I were."

Jim agreed with her. "They kept their fires going all the time. Gosh, they didn't even have matches to start it again if it went out. You know that, Nat."

Nat stood up. He wasn't going to admit that Barbara and Pat and Jim were right and he was wrong. "Battle stations, men," he coldly announced. "Johnny, back to the woodbin. Jim, are you working with me on this wall or — "

But Barbara was talking again and Jim was listening. "The fact is," she continued, "the treasure doesn't have to be in this room at all."

Not in this room? "What do you mean?" Nat growled.

Barbara smiled sweetly. " 'Taking care not to burn your hands,' " she quoted. "Near a fireplace, yes. But there are plenty of other fireplaces in this house. Who says it has to be in the kitchen?"

Barbara had won the argument. Nat wouldn't say so, but he headed the procession as the treasure hunters picked up their flashlights to walk through the rest of the house. All of them except Pat knew what they would find. There was a good-sized fireplace in the dining room, and two smaller fireplaces in the bedrooms directly overhead. There were no fireplaces on the other side of the house, not in the living room nor in the front bedroom upstairs, where George Washington had once slept.

That meant one, two, three, four places where Deborah had to take care not to burn her hands. Finding the treasure was going to be a big job.

12 | Treasure Hunting

THE LONG JULY DAYS PASSED QUICKLY. Every morning the boys and girls worked in the old house. They sprawled on the hearths and they poked at the walls. They pried out loose bricks and some that weren't quite so loose. In the afternoons, when they were tired of treasure hunting, they went swimming and played games like "King on the Mountain" and ball.

Whatever part of the day it was, they squabbled. Pat had never heard so many arguments in her whole life. Usually it was Nat or Barbara who started them.

Only this morning Nat was fooling around with his ruler at the fireplace wall in the kitchen. Standing up straight, he stretched out one arm until his

93

fingertips touched the brick. Then he began measuring above his hand.

"What in tarnation do you think you're doing?" Johnny wanted to know.

"What's the ruler for?" Barbara asked.

Nat turned his head toward Barbara. "You're so smart. How come you don't know?" When she didn't answer, he was glad to explain: "If I were going to hide a treasure, I'd put it in the most convenient place for me to reach. Where I wouldn't have to stand on tiptoe or stoop down. Right about so." With the ruler, he pointed to the bricks that his fingertips were touching.

"But —" Sam started to ask a question.

"Since I'm five foot six," Nat continued, "and Great-grandpa Woodruff must have been six feet tall at least, he'd have hidden it higher. Say six inches higher. Right about so." This time the ruler pointed farther up the wall. "Pretty clever, huh?" Smiling triumphantly, Nat scratched a brick with the corner of his ruler and started to lift it out.

"Pretty clever." Barbara mimicked him. "If I was going to hide a treasure I'd put it in the most convenient place for *me* to reach. And since I'm four feet ten, I'd put it here." Her fingertips touched a spot on the wall that was level with her shoulder.

"How do you know Woodruff was six feet tall?" she challenged. "Maybe he was a shrimp like me."

"I *know!*" Nat refused to discuss the matter further. He took out the brick he had marked, and hopefully flashed his light into the empty space. But there was no sign of a treasure there.

"Besides," Barbara continued, "maybe he put it in the most convenient place for Deborah. So she wouldn't have to stand on tiptoe. After all, that's what any gentleman would have done." With a toss of her head, she picked up the ruler and poked it into the crumbling clay — at her own shoulder height.

Six-footer, shrimp, or courtly gentleman? What manner of man was Great-grandpa Woodruff anyway? No one knew. Loyally, Pat stooped over to follow Barbara's lead. Loyally, Jim and Johnny stretched up their arms and bent back their heads to imitate Nat. Only Sam was in trouble. His heart was with his big brother, but his arms were too short.

Working morning after morning, the treasure hunters removed bricks from the kitchen fireplace until the wall looked like a checkerboard. Then they turned to the fireplaces in the bedrooms. Soon they had two squads at work, one to take out

95

bricks and the other to put them back. But no matter how many bricks they took out and how many they put back, they were no closer to finding a hollow space or a tin postbox.

"There's still the dining room," Nat sighed. "That's *got* to be the one."

The dining-room fireplace was different from the others. It was also lined with brick, with a stone hearth in front that opened out into the room. But the walls surrounding it were covered with wood. Broad panels of pine that dated way back to Great-grandpa Woodruff's time.

"How can you tell they're that old?" Pat asked.

"The nails, stupid." All the Paine boys knew the answer, and even Jim and Barbara joined the chorus. "They're handmade. Anybody knows that."

Pat ran her fingers across the satin-smooth panels and stared at the nails which fastened them to the wall. They had square, flat heads, and they seemed much bigger than the ones in her house.

She wanted to ask more about them, but she didn't dare. Nat was thumping the boards above the fireplace, listening for a hollow sound, and Jim was tapping the panels along the sides, hoping that one would slide open, the way secret panels do in books. But the wood continued to sound the way wood does when it's hit with a fist. And if there were sliding panels, Jim didn't discover them.

"If there's a treasure in this fireplace, we aren't going to find it without a hatchet." Jim straightened up and wiped the perspiration from his forehead.

"A hatchet!" Nat glared. He moved his fist from the pine panels above the fireplace, as if he were aiming it at Jim.

"Gosh, I was only joking." Jim defended himself. "Can't you take a joke?"

That was the trouble. Pat sighed. Nat couldn't take a joke. The treasure hunt, which had started out as an exciting game for everyone, was deadly serious for him.

As the days turned into weeks, the excitement began to wear off. Even Johnny and Sam were tired of taking out bricks and putting them back, and never finding one single thing.

One boiling-hot morning, the treasure hunters decided to go to the beach instead of working in the old house. All the boys and girls went to the beach except Nat. The whole time that they were swimming and splashing each other and burying their legs in the sand, he tramped up and down the stairs. He pried out bricks and hunted for hollow spaces behind the paneled walls.

Late in the afternoon, Pat walked over to bring him some orangeade that was left from the trip to the beach. He wasn't any farther along than he had been the day before, and he was tired and hot and cross.

"Pretty soon it'll be the first week in August." She tried to cheer him up. "Robert Popham said he was coming back then. Maybe he'll have some good ideas."

"Pretty soon it'll be August fifteenth," Nat pointed out, "and then *nobody's* ideas will be any good."

There was no use telling him that the world wasn't going to come to an end on the fifteenth of August, Pat thought. You couldn't blame him for feeling upset about losing the house. Studying the place from her bedroom window that evening, she could understand how he felt about it. With the moon shining on its roof and lighting up its windows, it didn't seem dilapidated or haunted any more. Or at least, if it was haunted, the ghosts weren't the scary kind who wore white sheets and moaned.

Pat could picture Deborah stirring a stew over the fire and putting a loaf of bread in the oven to bake. She could almost see her in the big front bedroom where George Washington slept, warming the general's sheets with a brass warming pan. Or outside, planting the rosebush by the kitchen window.

It was even easier to imagine Nathaniel, because so much of the house must have been the work of his two hands. Nathaniel hammering handmade nails into the pine boards in the dining room. Nathaniel carrying in the hearth stones and laying up the brick. Building the big fireplaces and the chimneys above them.

The chimneys! Pat almost pushed out the window screen in her excitement. Night after night she had looked across the field at the old house, but she had never noticed before that there were *two* chimneys rising from the roof: one on the side of the house nearest her, and one on the opposite side. One chimney for the fireplace in the kitchen and the fireplace in the dining room and the two bedroom fireplaces directly overhead, and one chimney which wasn't connected to any fireplaces at all!

This time it was Pat who started the chain of telephone calls — who called Nat who called Jim who called Barbara to say, "Meet in the garden right after breakfast. Pat's got an idea."

13 | The Missing Fireplaces

THE FOUR BOYS AND PAT WAITED in the garden until Barbara arrived. She biked down the path breathlessly, calling as she pedaled, "What is it? What did you find?"

But Pat was being mysterious. Instead of answering, she made everyone walk through the orchard and stand facing the house.

"Look," she commanded. "What do you see?"

They didn't see anything except the same old house that they had seen almost every day of their lives.

Nat scowled. "What do *you* see?" he asked.

"Chimneys." Pat was enjoying herself. "*Two* chimneys. Not one but two."

Nat stared at the roof. Then he streaked through the garden to the open kitchen window. Jim and Barbara were next, followed by Johnny and Sam. By the time Pat climbed in after them, everyone was racing around. They zigzagged in and out of the rooms on the far side of the broad central hall, and they scooted up the stairs to the bedrooms above. Of course they discovered, as they knew they would discover, that there were no fireplaces connected to the second chimney.

"There aren't any now," Pat said, as they sank to the floor of the big front bedroom to catch their breaths. "But there must have been fireplaces here once. When General Washington slept here, there must have been a fireplace in this room. Else his feet would have been awfully cold, even with a warming pan."

"General Washington slept here in July." Nat gloomily corrected her. "He'd have been hot, same as we are now."

But Pat wasn't going to let Nat spoil her big moment. She'd had time to think about the second chimney and the missing fireplaces. In the middle of the night, she had turned her desk lamp on and drawn a sketch of the house. Not a picture of the way it looked from the outside, but a plan showing how the rooms were arranged.

"See." She showed them her plan. "The kitchen and dining-room fireplaces are back to back. So are the ones above them. Four fireplaces, all connected to one chimney. Probably Nathaniel Woodruff built this side of the house the same way. Probably there was a fireplace right here." Walking across the room, she pointed to a spot in the middle of the wall.

The treasure hunters crowded around her. The wall looked like the paneled wall in the dining room. If there had been a fireplace, there was certainly no sign of it now.

Except — Nat stretched his neck forward to examine the middle panels. For the first time in weeks he came close to smiling.

"The nails," he said. "They're different. They're not handmade."

Pat looked too. So did Barbara and Jim and Johnny and Sam. The nailheads were round and regular, like the ones in the hardware store. There were uneven, square-headed nails in most of the paneling of the room, but right in the middle, where the fireplaces should have been, the nailheads were round!

"Great-grandpa built a fireplace here." Nat's voice was hoarse with excitement. "Then somebody else boarded it up. Maybe when they put in the furnace

102

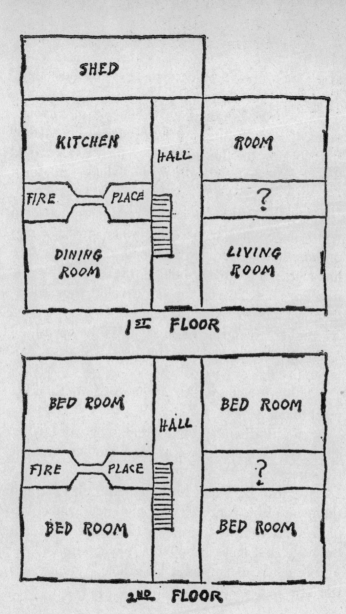

SHED

KITCHEN   HALL   ROOM

FIRE   PLACE   ?

DINING ROOM   LIVING ROOM

1ST FLOOR

BED ROOM   HALL   BED ROOM

FIRE   PLACE   ?

BED ROOM   BED ROOM

2ND FLOOR

and didn't need fireplaces to heat the house any more."

There wasn't any doubt about it in anyone's mind. The only question was, where should they start looking for the treasure? Which room should they tackle first? They zigzagged back and forth again, trying to decide.

The walls of the downstairs rooms were covered with plaster and paint. The walls of the rooms upstairs were covered with broad pine panels. The fireplaces were there, behind the paint and the paneling, but how in the world could they get at them without wrecking the house?

"Mother," Sam started to say. "We better ask —"

"Mother." Johnny shook his head. "She isn't going to like it."

"Mother!" Nat agreed, as he tried to think of what to do.

Jim and Barbara and Pat didn't say a word. After all, it wasn't *their* house, or *their* mother, or *their* treasure.

Nat paced back and forth, pounding his fist into the palm of his hand. "If we only knew which fireplace he'd hidden it in. We can't tear down all the walls, but if we knew exactly where to look —"

"We could make just a little hole," Johnny finished for him.

"Only so big." Sam held out his hands the way Robert had done when he described the tin box.

Jim slumped against the window. Barbara flopped down to the floor. Pat wrinkled her forehead and thought.

"I wonder," she suggested slowly. "Suppose we try an experiment, like dropping something down the chimney? A ball or something?"

"Suppose we did?"

"Well, maybe something would happen. We could listen to it fall, and maybe —"

"Maybe it would roll into a hollow space?" Johnny's eyes brightened.

"Maybe it would hit the tin box?" Sam lifted his head.

Nat stopped pacing and pounding his fist. He didn't think much of Pat's idea, but anything was worth trying. They didn't have many more days to hunt for Great-grandpa Woodruff's treasure.

"Jim —" He began to be bossy again. "You go home and get your baseball. I'll climb up on the roof and —"

"My baseball!" Jim protested. "What if it gets lost? It's easy enough to drop it down the chimney, but who's going to get it back?"

"Mine," Pat interrupted. "I mean my ball. It's

hard rubber, so we could hear it fall. And I don't really care if it gets lost."

Nat gave her a grateful look, and she headed for home. When she returned with the ball in her hand, everyone was arguing and complaining. Everyone wanted to go up on the roof and drop the ball down the chimney.

"I'm the oldest." Nat succeeded in shouting them down. "And the best climber. I'm going to drop the ball, and you're all going to listen to it fall. Jim —" He kept on being bossy. "You and Johnny take the two downstairs rooms. Pat and Barbara, you stay in the bedrooms up above."

"What about me?" Sam wanted to know.

Nat scratched his head. Where could Sam go? "The attic," he finally decided.

Sam frowned. He knew he was getting the worst assignment of all. Nothing was ever going to happen in the attic. But before he could protest, Nat issued his final commands.

"Signals, men. When I get up on the roof, when I'm standing by the chimney, I'll whistle good and loud. When I whistle, you start listening!"

14 | Listen!

Behind the kitchen, the shingled roof of the old house sloped almost to the ground. With the ball in his pocket, Nat boosted himself up and headed for the chimneys. It was like climbing a long, steep hill — a slippery, steep hill, without anything to hold on to for support. He walked upright at first, trying not to look down at the garden. After all, he was Nathaniel Woodruff Paine the Fourth, and he wasn't the least bit scared.

But as the roof grew steeper and he traveled farther and farther from the ground, he bent over. He lowered his head and stretched out his arms, until he was climbing on all fours. He was still Nathaniel Woodruff Paine the Fourth, but he climbed

107

up the slippery, steep roof as if he were a monkey heading for the top of a coconut palm.

The sun shone and the wind blew, and once Nat's foot slipped and he almost fell. At last, at long last, his hands closed around the ridgepole. From then on it was easy. Sitting astride the ridgepole, he slid over to the chimney. After catching his breath, he stood up and looked around. Jim and Johnny were watching him from the garden.

"How was it?" Jim shouted through cupped hands. "You all right?"

"Great," Nat puffed. "Easy as rolling off a log."

"Just what we were afraid of," Jim shouted back. "Say, what's it like in the chimney?"

Nat balanced himself carefully and peered down. "Dark," he yelled. "Hey, you two, how about getting inside? I don't want to stay up here all day."

Hugging the chimney stack, Nat waited while Jim and Johnny ran around to the front. When he heard the door slam, he fished the ball from his pocket. He counted up to ten slowly, so that they would have time to take their positions in the downstairs rooms.

Pat and Barbara were in the bedrooms, leaning

against the paneled walls. Sam was in the attic, wishing he were somewhere else. It was the first time that he'd ever been in the long, barnlike room when it was empty. It used to be crowded with trunks and ancient rocking chairs and picture frames. But all these had been moved out with the Paines, and now the room looked much as it must have looked in Great-grandpa Woodruff's time.

The ceiling sloped, and in parts of the room Sam had to be careful not to bump his head against low beams. On either side of him there was a broad column of brick. These were the chimneys which led from the fireplaces below to the roof where Nat was standing.

It was stifling hot in the attic, and the musty smell made Sam sneeze. He opened a little dirt-streaked window before taking his place next to one of the brick columns. He could hear Nat moving around overhead. He almost thought he could hear Nat's breathing.

On the roof, Nat finished counting. He put two fingers to his mouth and whistled as loud as he could. Then he dropped the ball into the chimney.

The ball fell, past Sam who was sneezing in the attic, past Pat and Barbara in the bedrooms underneath. At their stations on the first floor, Jim and

Johnny could hear it bounce and bounce and bounce again before it slowly rolled to a stop. They kept on listening, but that was all that they heard.

Nat sat down on the roof and started to slide. Braking himself with his hands, he slid slowly down, down, down, until he was close enough to the ground to jump. Then he ran around to the front of the house to find out what had happened.

In the living room, Jim and Johnny and Pat and Barbara were staring wide-eyed at the plaster wall.

"It's in there, all right." Johnny said. "We heard it."

"What's in there?" Nat's face lit up. "What did you hear?"

"The ball." Jim turned to answer him. "We heard it bounce."

"What did it sound like?" Nat grabbed his arm.

"Like — like a ball bouncing on the sidewalk."

"Not — not like a ball hitting a tin box?"

"Not like a ball hitting a tin box." Jim sighed.

The boys and girls looked from the wall to Nat and then back to the wall again. Their experiment had failed. They were sure now that there was a fireplace behind the plaster, but they were no closer to finding the treasure than they had ever been.

"Hey!" A cry from upstairs broke the silence.

111

Nat looked around. "Where's Sam?" he asked.

Sam wasn't there. Sam was standing at the head of the attic stairs, shouting at the top of his lungs. Had he discovered something? Everyone raced upstairs to find out.

Sam tossed back the lock of hair that was hanging in his eyes. "Wait'll you see it." He grinned.

"See what?" Nat grunted, hardly able to speak.

"See what?" Johnny demanded.

But Sam refused to be hurried by his brothers. Leading them into the attic, he sat down on the floor next to the chimney. "Ssh," he whispered with his finger on his lips. "Listen."

Everyone shushed. Everyone listened. There was a faint peeping, cheeping, twittering kind of noise.

"Now look." With the sleeve of his shirt, Sam brushed away some of the cobwebs which covered the chimney. Close to the attic floor, the chimney wasn't made of brick. Close to the attic floor, there was a little iron door.

While everyone stooped and squatted and pushed to get closer, Sam lifted the latch and opened the door. The peeping, cheeping, twittering noise grew louder. In the light filtering down from above, the treasure hunters could see that there was a shelf inside the chimney. A shelf with a nest of baby birds resting on it.

Nat sank back on his heels, speechless with disappointment.

"Birds," Jim sighed.

"Birds," Johnny echoed in disgust.

"Birds," Barbara complained.

Sam's face fell. He looked as if he were going to cry.

"What kind do you suppose they are?" Pat tried to cheer him up. She was interested in the birds even if nobody else was.

"Robins?" Sam guessed, feeling a little bit better.

"Swallows," Barbara corrected him. "Barn swallows, I'm pretty sure."

While Nat and Jim and Johnny sat without moving, Sam and the two girls took turns poking their heads in the little door to see the birds.

It was damp and spooky inside the chimney shaft, and Pat couldn't see very much. She put out her hand to feel the nest. She put out her hand, and felt dried grass and mud cemented together.

Behind the nest she felt something else — something that didn't belong to the swallows or to any other kind of bird. Her cheeks were scarlet when she pulled her head back into the room.

"Anybody go-got a fl-flashlight?" she stammered. "Th-there's *something on the shelf.*"

Everybody sprang into action. Everybody had a flashlight. Everybody pushed and shoved and tried to poke his head in the door. But there was only room for one head at a time, and it was Nat who got there first.

It was Nat who flicked his light from the baby birds in their nest to the shelf beyond. It was Nat who reached into the chimney, and Nat who backed out with a dusty box in his hand. A tin box that was just about the size and shape of a toolbox!

15 | The Book and Other Treasures

IF IT HAD BEEN HOT IN THE ATTIC BEFORE, it was stifling now. Only nobody seemed to care. Nobody complained. Nobody said a word.

Five heads turned in unison as Nat put the tin box down on the floor. Five mouths hung open as he lifted its lid. The first thing they saw was a book, a leather-covered book with gilt lettering on its worn binding.

"The book and other treasures," Johnny mumbled as Nat handed it to him to hold.

Underneath the book were folded sheets of paper, yellowed sheets with words written on them in faded blue ink. And beneath these, there was — money!

At least the boys and girls thought it was — hoped it was — money. The bills were big, much larger than the bills they were used to seeing, and they had crude pictures on them with funny, old-fashioned writing.

Nat picked one up and began to read out loud. "This Bill entitles the Bearer to receive Sixty Spanish Milled Dollars, or the Value thereof in Gold or Silver, according to a Resolution of Congress passed at Philadelphia, July 22, 1776." Only he read "refolution" and "paffed" because some of the s's looked like f's.

He read another and another and another. "This Bill entitles the Bearer to receive Five Spanish Milled Dollars . . . Forty-five Spanish Milled Dollars . . . Seven . . . Nine . . . Fifty . . ."

"Keen-o." Jim whistled softly.

"Cool, man," Johnny agreed.

"But do you suppose they're really real?" Sam asked. "They look like the play money you get at the five-and-ten."

" 'Course they're real," Nat said. He turned a bill around so that Sam could see "Continental Currency" printed on both its ends.

"Sixty, sixty-five, eighty-three — umm, a hundred and twenty-eight." Barbara was doing mental arithmetic, trying to add up the bills to see how much money they had found in the box.

Pretty soon everybody joined her. Everybody counted and added and got mixed up. Pretty soon the bills were scattered on the attic floor, and one of them was torn.

"That's enough." Nat angrily called for order by banging his fist on the lid of the box. "*I'll* count the money," he grandly announced. "Who's got a pencil?"

Pockets were turned inside out, but nobody had a pencil. At last Pat produced a scrap of blue chalk. With the floor as her slate, she copied the numbers that Nat read from the bills. Nat added, Pat added, Jim added. Even Sam went over the column of figures until they were all agreed. They had found $631.

No one had ever seen such an enormous sum of money before. Pat's eyes traveled from the chalk marks on the floor to Nat's face. Surely he would manage a smile now.

But Nat figured the Continental dollars and shook his head. "It's not enough. Not half enough to save the house. We need thousands, Mother said."

"But maybe the money's worth more now because it's so old," Jim suggested. "You know, like stamps. I've got a five-cent stamp in my album that's worth a quarter because it's eighty years old. These bills are even older than that."

"Maybe." There was a thoughtful gleam in Nat's eyes. "Maybe. We'll have to find out."

Barbara was getting restless. " 'The book and other treasures' — we haven't even looked at them yet."

At some other time, in some other place, the book would have been interesting. It was a dictionary, *Attick's New Spelling Dictionary*, the title page said, "printed in London in 1775." Its covers were warped, and there were spots of mold on the binding, but right on the very first page there was a name written in a flowing, old-fashioned script. The name was Nathaniel Woodruff.

"It's 'the book,' all right — the book he left for his son." Pat was excited.

"But it's only a book," Nat sighed. "After all, it can't be worth a lot — not thousands of dollars, anyway."

The book was only a book, but the folded sheets of paper were something else again. At first glance they seemed to be letters with addresses written on the outside of each sheet. But what did the addresses mean?

The top three letters — if they were letters — were addressed to "TRARENY JNFUVATGBA," and the next two said "ZNWBE GNYYZNQTR." The treasure hunters laughed as they tried to pronounce the words.

"They're Russian," Pat guessed.

"African," Jim said.

Then everyone stopped laughing. Because the last sheet of paper, the one on the bottom of the pile, was different. The handwriting of the address was old, like the signature in the dictionary, but it wasn't hard to read.

"For my beloved son Nathaniel," it said. Nat's fingers shook as he unfolded the yellowed paper to read the message. Then his face fell.

The letter didn't make sense at all. "FNZHRY

ZBEEVF 182-14 47-3 272-7," it started. The rest was all numbers separated by little dashes, with "G.W." written at the end.

All of the other papers contained the same sort of message, mostly numbers, with a few letters at the beginning and the end, but nothing that the boys and girls could understand. It wasn't Russian. It wasn't African.

"It's a code." Jim breathed the word lovingly.

"They're clues." Sam nodded his head.

"Clues to what?" Johnny asked.

"To where the treasure is hidden," Sam explained. "Don't you remember the treasure hunt we had at the 'Y' last year? First you find one clue. Then that one tells you where to find the next one. After you've found about a dozen clues, you get the treasure."

Barbara exchanged glances with Pat. Pat looked sideways at Nat. It had taken them weeks to find the tin box, and there wasn't much time left.

"But this *is* the treasure," Jim argued with Sam. "Or at least that's what Nathaniel Woodruff called it. 'The book and such other treasures as are in the old postbox.'"

"There's more to it than this. There's *got* to be

more," Nat insisted. "We just have to find out what these mean."

He looked so troubled that Pat took the six pieces of paper and spread them out on the floor. By the light of their flashlights, they studied the meaningless jumble of numbers and foreign-looking words.

"They are letters," Barbara decided after a few minutes. "Look. All of them except the 'my son Nathaniel' one begin with a whatchemecallit — a greeting — and end with a signature."

"But —"

"But —"

"But —"

"But how many buts make a goat?" Barbara sounded annoyed. "Look," she repeated. "Three of the letters start 'TRARENY JNFUVATGBA,' and two 'ZNWBE GNYYZNQTR,' just like the writing on the envelopes. And they all end the same way: 'FNZHRY ZBEEVF. FNZHRY' " — she twisted her tongue around, trying to pronounce the word — "whoever he was, wrote all these letters."

"Except the one to 'my son,' " Pat pointed out. "That's from G.W., and —"

"If FNZHRY wrote the letters," Nat interrupted "then FNZHRY must mean Nathaniel Woodruff."

"Couldn't." Barbara contradicted him. "Doesn't make any sense."

"Why not?" Nat looked as if he was going to get angry.

"Because the name is too short. FNZHRY ZBEEVF" — she counted rapidly on her fingers — "has twelve letters, and Nathaniel Woodruff has — um — seventeen. Gosh, Nat, we've made up codes millions of times. You ought to know how they work by now," she scolded.

Nat frowned. Instead of answering her, he picked up the letters — if they were letters — and put them in the tin box, on top of the Continental dollars and the dictionary. Then he closed the lid of the box.

"Hey," Jim asked, "where do you think you're going?"

"Home," Nat announced. "To figure out the code."

"By yourself?"

"It's not fair."

"You can't do that."

"We found it too."

Suddenly it was hot in the attic, stifling hot. Sam sneezed and Jim mopped his forehead with the sleeve of his shirt. It was hot and noisy in the low-ceilinged room.

Nat walked to the head of the stairs with the tin box tucked under his arm. "All right," he grudgingly agreed. "You can all have a chance. I'll give you — lend you — each a letter to work on. But you'd better take good care of it. We'll see who's the first to break the code."

16 | Alphabet Soup

"LET'S EAT LUNCH AT MY PLACE," Pat suggested, as she and Barbara walked through the garden of the old house. "Mom went over to Grandma's, but she said she'd leave hard-boiled eggs and stuff."

"Uh huh." Barbara absent-mindedly agreed.

She wasn't even thinking about lunch. She was thinking about ciphers and codes and spies. But when they reached the Harrison kitchen, the eggs looked good. While Pat chopped them up in a little chopping jar, Barbara spread bread with mayonnaise and fixed a pitcher of ice-cold lemonade.

They decided to eat under the big oak tree, where it was shady and cool. It took several trips before they had everything ready — sandwiches, paper cups, lemonade, and a bowl full of peaches and plums.

Barbara sank down on the grass and then sat up again. "Our letters," she moaned. "We left them on the kitchen counter. Gosh, if anything happens to them —"

"I'll get them," Pat offered. "You wait here."

She ran back to the kitchen. Where could she put the letters so that they wouldn't get dirty or anything? After thinking about it for a moment, she took two big books from the living-room shelves and tucked the letters between their pages. Then she borrowed paper and pencils from Mother's desk. When they were finished eating, they would be all ready for an afternoon of work.

"The way I see it" — Barbara waved her sandwich in the air — "it'll be a cinch to solve the alphabet code. It's those numbers I'm worrying about."

"What's a cinch about FNZHRY ZBEEVF?" Pat groaned. "He sounds awful to me." She had never solved a code or even looked at one before. This seemed to be another thing that people in Haven did and New Yorkers knew nothing about.

"Old FNZHRY probably just turned the alphabet around, so that Z stood for A and Y for B and X for C." Barbara paused to swallow her last bite of sandwich. "Or he switched every second letter, so that B stood for A and D for C, like that. Gosh, there are a million different ways he could have done it."

Pat had only a faint idea of what Barbara was talking about. Using one of the big books to lean on, she wrote the alphabet, one letter under another, down the side of a piece of paper. Then, more slowly, because it was hard to think of the letters backward she put Z next to A and Y next to B and X next to C, until she had a second column alongside the first one:

A Z
B Y
C X
D W

"Like that?" she asked. When Barbara nodded, she stared down at the paper. "So if I wanted to write Pat in code I'd write KZG?"

"Exactly." Barbara agreed. "See how easy it is?"

"But if you have words like FNZHRY, and you don't know what code he used, how do you figure it out?"

"That's simple too." Barbara reached for a plum. "You know that stuff about how the letter E is used

most often, and the next one is T and then A, don't
you?"

Pat shook her head. At this moment she felt as
if she didn't know anything at all.

Sighing, Barbara wiped plum juice from her chin.
"There's a whole list like that in a book about codes
in the library. You count the different letters in
your code message. So if you have fifty-five V's
and forty G's and thirty Z's, then you know V is E
and G is T —"

"And Z is A." Pat was studying her columns of
letters. "So you know the code is just the alphabet
backward. Now I get it."

It was easy to "get it" when Barbara talked, but
harder when they looked at the messages that Nat
had given them. Pat's letter began with TRARENY
JNFUVATGBA. After that came eight lines of
numbers, just plain numbers, then two shorter
lines:

LBHE BORQVRAG FREINAG
FNZHRY ZBEEVF

Barbara's letter started ZNWBE GNYYZNQTR,
followed by seven lines of numbers and the same
unpronounceable signature.

"If it is a signature," Pat pointed out.

128

"Got to be." There wasn't any doubt about it in Barbara's mind. "All the letters end the same way, except the one to 'my son.' Gosh, I wonder who G.W. is."

"Maybe the W stands for Woodruff," Pat suggested.

"Could be," Barbara agreed. She reached for a pencil and a piece of paper. "No use worrying about that now. Let's count the different letters."

Both girls counted and scribbled and chewed on the ends of their pencils. Something was wrong. There wasn't any letter that was used lots more often than any other. Pat counted seven R's, but there were only five in Barbara's message. And she had five N's and five E's too.

"You know what I think?" Barbara asked. "I think we just don't have a long enough message to work with. I think that book on codes said you had to have fifty words anyway, and we only have fourteen."

"Really only nine," Pat sighed. "Because so many of the words are the same."

"You know what I think?" Barbara repeated. "I think we have to guess. I mean, you try the alphabet backward, and I'll try switching every second letter and see what happens."

Pat picked up her pencil and started translating. If A was Z and B was Y, then TRARENY was —

"GIZIVMB." She tried to pronounce the word. "That can't be right."

"Mine doesn't work either," Barbara said, "but there are lots more ways to do it. Begin in the middle of the alphabet this time."

Pat wrinkled up her nose. "What do you mean?"

Grabbing Pat's piece of paper, Barbara started a third column of letters. "A is N," she impatiently explained. "B is O, C is P. Keep on going like that until you've written down the whole alphabet. Then see if it works."

Laboriously, Pat copied down the letters as Barbara had told her to. They were beginning to swim around on her paper, the way letters do when you eat alphabet soup. If the truth were to be told, she was a little bit tired of this game in which Barbara was so fast and she was so slow.

Her fingers grasped her pencil tightly as she started translating. "TRARENY. T is G. R is E. A is N," she mumbled. Then she grabbed Barbara's arm. "Look! Look — it spells —"

"GENERAL!" Barbara yelled. "Oh boy, we're getting it."

Pat forgot about being tired as she translated the next word. Instead, cold shivers ran up and down her spine. TRARENY JNFUVATGBA meant GENERAL WASHINGTON!

Barbara reached up to the lowest limb of the oak tree and chinned herself three times. Pat sat still and blinked her eyes. She felt as if she were traveling backward in a time machine. The letter on her lap, the letter that she had offhandedly left on the kitchen counter a little while before, had been written to George Washington!

Inside the house the telephone rang. Shaking herself so that she could come back to the present day again, she ran up the front steps to answer it.

"Pat?" It was Jim's voice at the other end of the wire.

"Jim!" Pat breathlessly answered.

"The letter I have —"

"The letter Nat gave me —"

At the same moment, both of them shouted into their receivers: *"It's addressed to General Washington!"*

17 | I Care About Old Books

WHOOPING WITH EXCITEMENT, the boys ran up New Street to join Pat and Barbara under the oak tree. It was only a few minutes work to figure out the rest of the words in the message. If TRARENY JNFUVATGBA was General Washington, then ZNWBE GNYYZNQTR was Major Tallmadge, whoever he was. The signatures on the messages were all the same: "Your obedient servant, Samuel Morris."

It was only a few minutes work to figure out this much, but that was all that the boys and girls could decipher. Nat and Jim and Johnny and Sam and Barbara stretched out on their stomachs on the grass, with pads and pencils in front of them.

They tried all sorts of ways to make sense out of the numbers.

"Suppose 1 stands for A, 2 stands for B . . . Suppose 10 stands for A, 20 stands for B . . . Or 1 stands for Z and 2 for Y . . ."

Pat sat up, leaning against the trunk of the oak tree, with her papers and book in her lap. This was even worse than alphabet soup. For this, you needed one of those mechanical brains. Or any kind of brain except her own, which didn't want to work at all.

Closing her eyes, she listened to the rustling leaves over her head and tried not to listen to the arguments taking place on the grass at her feet. Pretty soon her time machine shifted into gear again. Drowsily, she thought about General Washington. Washington with his powdered wig and buckled shoes. Washington standing up in a rowboat as he crossed the Delaware. Washington maybe right here in Haven, climbing up to the attic of the old house next door. Only it was a new house then.

"How do you suppose he knew where to look for the letters?" she asked.

"He?"

"Who?"

"What are you talking about?"

The others sounded annoyed at her interruption. And they weren't pleased when Pat explained that she had been thinking about Washington walking up the attic stairs to collect his mail.

She closed her eyes again, but her dream was spoiled. The time machine refused to budge. She was back in the present, sitting under the oak tree, with a job to be done.

Opening the book on her lap, she looked once more at the letter that had been written to General Washington. "352-10 200-8 182-5." What could these numbers mean? They looked as if someone had been fooling with an adding machine.

Her eyes traveled from the letter to the open pages of the book. It showed a picture of an old house, a house and some furniture from Colonial times. She turned to another page, hoping that no one would notice that she wasn't working on the code.

The book was really interesting. It described how the houses were built, and the kinds of chairs and tables and beds people used in the olden days. There were pictures of fireplaces and spinning wheels and square-headed, handmade nails. There was even a picture of a chimney with a little iron door in it, like the iron door in the attic of the Paine House.

"Hey," she called to the code-solvers, "I found something."

When the boys and Barbara raised their heads, she showed them the picture and started reading the words underneath. "Smoke oven in attic. Meat was often hung in the chimney so that the smoke from the fireplaces below could be used to cure it. The door —"

No one would let her finish. Even Barbara didn't want to hear about smoke ovens and curing meat. Even Jim frowned at her. Nat didn't frown. He positively glared.

"Do you know what day it is?" he asked through clenched teeth. "It's the first of August — and you sit around reading. Who cares about an old book anyway?"

"I do," Pat loftily replied. Most of the time, she remembered that she felt sorry for Nat, but this afternoon she was hot and headachy. It was her turn to act cross. "I care about old books," she announced in her most grown-up, city-girl manner. "In fact, I'd like to see the old dictionary."

"Why?" Nat wanted to know, as he opened the tin box. "Why?" he repeated, as he handed her the book.

"I am sure it's full of clues." Pat tilted up her nose and tossed back her head.

"What kind of clues?" Barbara asked.

"What kind of clues?" Jim queried.

"What kind of clues?" Nat growled.

But all Pat would say was, "Never mind. You'll find out." All Pat *could* say was "Never mind," because she hadn't the ghost of an idea about the dictionary. Her talk about clues was pure bluff.

While the others went back to work on their numbers, she slumped against the tree, leafing through the dictionary. Whatever had possessed her to talk as if she knew something about it? Turning the yellowed pages, with a pencil in her hand, she pretended to be busy.

It was a dictionary all right, not very different from present-day ones, except for those funny *s*'s that were written like *f*'s. Idly, she hunted for different words: "leaf" and "oak" and "tree." Right above "tree," there was "treasure."

What was it that Nathaniel Woodruff had written to his wife? "The book and such other treasures." He didn't say, "The book and the treasure." He said, "The book and such other treasures," as if — as if the book itself was a treasure.

Pat straightened up abruptly, forgetting about the heat and her aching head. Maybe the dictionary really was a clue. Maybe the key to the code was hidden between its covers!

She studied the leather binding carefully, hoping to find an opening, a place where a message might be concealed. Then she turned the book upside down. Holding it by its covers, she shook it vigorously. But no papers fluttered to the ground.

"What in heck do you think you're doing?" Nat exploded. "If you care so much about old books, what's the idea of trying to tear it to pieces?"

"No idea at all." Pat shrugged her shoulders. "I'm only looking for the key to the code, that's all. It's in the dictionary, I'm sure."

There she went again! Why had she said such a thing? She wasn't the least bit sure about the code or the dictionary or practically anything. The boys and Barbara didn't know this, of course. They dropped their pencils and pads, and took turns examining the old book. They flipped through the pages, and they fingered the binding. They held the book upside down, until it threatened to give way at the seams.

"Hey," Nat protested. "That's no way to do it. If there is a key there, it's probably glued in so it won't fall out. Have to look at every single page."

"Did they have glue in the olden days?" Sam wondered.

"Naw," Johnny joked. "They fastened everything with Scotch tape."

Ignoring his brothers, Nat took the book from Barbara and began leafing through it, page by page. Without thinking, he started to count pages under his breath. "Forty-one, forty-two, forty-three, forty-four . . ." The others watched impatiently as he droned on and on and on.

"Ugh, numbers!" Barbara complained. "I am so sick of numbers, I could scream."

"Numbers!" Something clicked inside Pat's head. She pointed a shaking forefinger at the book. "The dictionary's full of numbers — numbers on every page. All the way from 1 to 400 and something."

Nat stared at her. Jim sank back on his heels, trying to figure out what she meant. Barbara squealed, as she suddenly understood. Snatching the dictionary from Nat's hand, she read aloud from her letter.

"It says '411–9.' "

"Look on page 411," Pat commanded in a husky voice.

"Line 9," Nat shouted, as he too caught on.

Barbara turned pages as fast as she could. "Page 411, line 9," she repeated. "The word is 'troops.' "

Suddenly it was so quiet under the oak tree that you could have heard an eraser drop on the grass. Or the sound of a butterfly's fluttering wings.

"Go on," Nat croaked.

"Okay, 255–12," Barbara read. "Page 255, line 12, is 'moving'; 404–3: 'to'; 230–7: 'long'; 213–14: 'island.' *Troops moving to Long Island.*" Her eyes were round as saucers as she translated the first sentence of the letter in her lap.

"Gad, sir!" Sam broke the silence.

After that everyone whooped and hollered and yelled, until they could be heard way down on Old Post Road. The numbered pages of the dictionary were the key to the code!

18 | Master Spy or Master Thief?

WITH PAT AND THE BOYS breathing down her neck and peering over her shoulder, Barbara continued her translation. Troops were moving to Long Island, and a fleet was making ready to sail to the Virginia Capes. " 'Which,' " she read out loud, as if she were reciting in school, " 'will leave the enemy garrison in weakened condition. The time will soon be aus-' " — she stumbled over the word — " 'auspicious for His Excellency's return to the city. Your obedient servant, Samuel Morris.' "

"Who's 'His Excellency'?" Sam wanted to know. "King George?"

"King George!" Johnny spluttered. "You crazy or something? Morris was telling the Americans that the time was aus-—aus-—ripe to recapture New York. 'His Excellency' must have been Washington."

Sam pouted. "How do you know?"

Before the discussion could develop into an argument, Pat asked for the dictionary. But Nat had already taken the old book from Barbara's lap.

"First 'my son Nathaniel,' " he announced.

Pat nodded. She couldn't blame Nat for wanting to read that letter first. As he read the words from the dictionary, she wrote them down:

"Samuel Morris has been of the utmost service to our cause. Time and again the intelligence he has procured has saved our forces. Of his fidelity and ability, I entertain the highest opinion. When these trying times are done with, he shall receive his just reward from his grateful countrymen. G. W."

"Spy." Jim mouthed the word lovingly. "Samuel Morris was an American spy."

"Just like Nathan Hale." Johnny smiled. " 'I regret that I have only one life —' "

"Better than Nathan Hale," Barbara announced.

Only Nat was silent, concentrating on the letter with a puzzled frown. "What does this have to do with 'my son Nathaniel'?" he wondered aloud, "Who *was* Samuel Morris, anyway?"

Before anyone could answer — if they had known what to say — Mrs. Harrison's car turned into the driveway. Nat closed the dictionary and started folding up the letters.

"Not a word now," he warned. "My mother's going to be the first one to hear about this. She's got a right."

By the time Mrs. Harrison had parked the car and closed the garage door and walked over to say hello, the letters were out of sight. Nat was squatting on the grass, hiding the tin box behind him, and Barbara was talking with Johnny about popular songs.

"My, it's hot." Mrs. Harrison smiled. "Who'd like to come inside for some soda or lemonade?"

Nat stood up and awkwardly backed away from the oak tree. "Thanks all the same," he said, "but I have to go now. Have a lot of work to do."

Johnny and Sam followed their brother's lead, and Jim soon remembered that he had promised his mother to come home early. Which left Barbara and Pat to drink the soda that Mrs. Harrison had brought and to argue about hit tunes. All the time they were talking about records and singers, they were thinking about the Paines and Jim — and Samuel Morris and General Washington.

It wasn't until they all met in the kitchen of

the old house the next morning that the girls learned what was in the other letters. Every message was full of news about New York and Long Island in the spring of 1781.

" 'The English fleet of transports and merchantmen of about seventy sail left Sandy Hook the middle of last week. . . . A private ship arrived from England on Friday last with the king's speech. . . . The enemy papers give a large account of Arnold's success in the South. . . .' "

"Read this one." Jim handed a letter to Pat. "This one's cool. It tells how Morris almost got captured because someone informed against him and he had to hide in the woods —"

"And cross over from Long Island at night in a fishing boat," Johnny interrupted.

"You kids act as if this was a television show," Nat complained.

"Gosh, it would be real neat on TV. 'Samuel Morris, Master Spy,' " Sam said in a creepy voice.

Pat started to giggle, until she saw the expression on Nat's face. "Look," he said. "These letters are great and all that, but has it occurred to any of you that it is now August second. We've found Nathaniel Woodruff's postbox all right, and his book and —"

"And $630," Jim reminded him.

"No, $631," Johnny corrected.

Nat frowned at the interruptions. "But that *can't* be all the treasure he left for his son."

"Maybe somebody stole the rest," Sam suggested.

"Who?" Before anyone else had a chance, Nat answered his own question. "I'll tell you who. It was Samuel Morris."

"You're crazy, man."

"Stark raving mad."

Nat waited for the storm to die down. "It had to be Morris," he insisted. "What are his letters doing in our house anyway? How come it's Samuel Morris' letters that are in Great-grandpa Woodruff's postbox? The fact is, your wonderful master spy was a master thief."

"Im-possible." A deep voice boomed from the open window. A man was standing outside. A man was lifting his leg over the sill. A man was climbing into the kitchen to join them. He looked like — he couldn't be —

"Robert!" Pat and Barbara shouted in chorus.

Sam walked over to him and pointed a finger at his face. "You haven't any beard," he said, accusingly.

"No beard at all," Robert agreed. "I shaved it off. Too hot for summer. What's this I hear?" He turned

to Nat. "You found some letters from Samuel Morris?"

"Spy letters!"

"And the book."

"And the postbox."

"And $631."

"Only that's not enough."

"Not enough?" Robert turned his head from one to the other as they spoke. "Sounds as if you'd found enough for a hundred kids."

"Why'd you say 'impossible' when you were outside?" Nat asked. "What's so great about Samuel Morris?"

"He was only a leader in George Washington's Secret Service, that's all," Robert answered. "Just one of the men Washington most relied on after the British took New York."

" 'Time and again the intelligence he has procured has saved our forces,' " Barbara quoted.

"Where did you get that from?" Robert sounded excited.

"From one of the letters we found," Barbara explained. "The one from Washington."

Robert swallowed hard. Robert blinked. "You — you kids found a letter from Washington? George Washington?"

"And three letters from Samuel Morris, addressed to Washington." Nat nodded. "They were right here all the time in Great-grandpa Woodruff's tin box."

Robert turned red and white and red again as he looked through the box and read the translations of the code letters. After he was finished, he insisted on going upstairs to see the smoke oven. The baby birds were still there, chirping and cheeping and twittering. When Robert put his hand behind their nest to make sure that there weren't any more boxes lying on the shelf, a mother bird swooped down from the roof, trying to chase him away.

Back in the kitchen, he stroked his chin and once more went over the contents of the tin box. He carried the dictionary over to the window to look at the signature on the first page of the book. Then he examined each letter in the same way.

The boys and girls were bursting with curiosity. At last Nat could contain himself no longer. "Why," he demanded to know, "are Samuel Morris' letters in Nathaniel Woodruff's box?"

Robert hesitated. "I think — Remember, I'm not positive — I'm pretty sure, though —"

"Tell us!" everyone shouted.

147

"I'm pretty sure," Robert continued, "that Samuel Morris' letters were in Nathaniel Woodruff's box because Samuel Morris and Nathaniel Woodruff were the same man. I think — it's a pretty good guess — that Great-grandpa Woodruff was Washington's chief spy!"

19 | A Smile from Nat

T HIS TIME ROBERT WAS CHAIRMAN of the meeting in the kitchen. This time Robert did the talking, and even Nat sat crosslegged on the floor and listened to him.

"Way after the Revolution," he explained, "Major Tallmadge wrote a book telling about Washington's spies. He published a number of letters from Samuel Morris — the same kind of letters you found — besides stuff from Washington praising his work."

"But who was Major Tallmadge?" Barbara interrupted.

"Benjamin Tallmadge. He was in charge of Washington's Secret Service," Robert replied. "It was his job to find the spies and arrange the codes and all. He was stationed right around here during most of the Revolution, which is how I happened to read his book. He helped uncover Benedict Arnold's plot and capture Major André. You know all about that, of course."

Of course. Nat and Barbara and Jim nodded wisely. Pat didn't nod. She had only a faint suspicion that Benedict Arnold was bad, and as for Major André —

"The one thing Tallmadge never revealed and historians have always wondered about," Robert continued, "was the identity of Samuel Morris."

"Identity?" Sam tugged at his wandering lock of hair.

"Who he was," Robert explained. "None of the spies used their real names in their letters, for fear that the British would find them out."

"You mean" — Johnny suddenly understood — "Samuel Morris was just a name he took, like — like Zorro?"

"Like Robin Hood," Jim added.

"Like Zorro. Like Robin Hood," Robert agreed. "Samuel Morris has always been a mystery man —"

"Until today," Barbara pointed out. "Until we solved the mystery."

"Remember, we're not positive yet," Robert warned. "We still have to prove that Morris and Woodruff were the same man."

"How are we going to do that?" Sam wondered. "Fingerprints?"

"I don't know about fingerprints, whether they'd keep for one hundred and eighty years," Robert said. "But we've got something even better —"

"Handwriting!" Nat and Pat guessed at the same moment.

Nat reached for the letter addressed to "my son Nathaniel." Pat turned to the first page of the dictionary where "Nathaniel Woodruff" was inscribed. Barbara unfolded one of the Samuel Morris letters.

" 'Course it's the same."

"Look at those skinny *a*'s."

"And the way he wrote *l*."

"Looks the same to me," Robert admitted, "but we don't know for sure that Nathaniel Woodruff addressed that letter to his son or signed his name in the dictionary."

Nat frowned. He was ready for an argument until he remembered something. "The letter to Deborah — the letter telling about the treasure in the old postbox — that *has* to be in his writing."

"Right." Robert nodded. "I was just going to suggest that I drive over to the college library with these" — he waved toward the tin box and its contents — "and compare them with the Woodruff letter there."

"I'll go with you," Nat informed him.

"Take me," Johnny begged.

"Me!" Sam insisted.

Pat and Jim and Barbara didn't say a word. They looked so appealingly at Robert that he couldn't turn them down.

Ten minutes later the six boys and girls were tiptoeing down the stairs of York University's library. Twenty minutes later they were hopping up and down, their voices echoing in the basement room, as Robert tried vainly to quiet them.

It didn't take a handwriting expert to see that the Nathaniel who'd signed the letter to his wife, Deborah, was the same Nathaniel who'd written in the dictionary and who'd signed "Samuel Morris" to the letters to Tallmadge and Washington. It didn't take a detective to figure out that Samuel Morris really was Nathaniel Woodruff.

Back in the kitchen of the old house, Robert shook Nat's hand. "Congratulations, my son Na-

thaniel." He smiled. "How does it feel to be the great-great-— how many greats are there? — grandson of George Washington's chief spy? Pretty proud of Grandpa now, aren't you?"

For a moment, Nat didn't answer. He was pleased, of course. But after all, he had always been proud of Nathaniel Woodruff. He had always known that he was a remarkable man. "The treasure," he sighed. "It still won't be enough to save the house. Only $631, and we have to have thousands."

"$631? How do you figure that?" Robert asked.

"The money — here." Johnny took the pile of bills from the tin box and waved them at Robert.

Robert clapped his hand to his forehead. "But that's Continental money," he laughed. "You kids don't expect to spend that, do you?"

"I thought it was play money too when I first looked at it," Sam informed him. "But when you read the writing on it, you can see —"

Robert stopped laughing and started to groan. "Haven't you ever heard the expression, 'not worth a Continental'? Even during the Revolution, this money wasn't worth more than a few pennies. By the end of the war, people were using the bills to paper their walls. Today — well, I suppose you

could get a couple of dollars apiece from a collec-
tor —"

"Even for the sixty-dollar one?" Johnny sounded
as if he didn't believe him.

"I'm no expert on old money," Robert said, "but I
bet you couldn't get more than two or three dollars
for it, and maybe less. But my gosh, that's not
important —"

"Not important?" Nat burst out. "Don't you suppose we'd like to live here, in Nathaniel Woodruff's
house, instead of that dinky little place down the
street?"

"Not important? Maybe not to you," Johnny
scolded.

"Not important —" Sam began.

"*Not important.*" Robert shouted the words so
that everyone would hear him and keep quiet
while he talked. "Not important, because you've
got your treasure right here in this tin box. The spy
letters that Woodruff wrote and the letter from
General Washington. I'll bet that there are dozens
of places where you could sell them — museums,
libraries, private collectors."

"How much" — Nat hesitated — "how much
would they pay?"

"It would certainly be in the thousands. Enough to pay the back taxes, and even" — Robert looked around the kitchen — "buy some cement to hold those bricks in place."

Nat opened his mouth, but no words came out. Instead, the corners of his lips turned up and up and up, until a broad smile stretched across his face. It was the second of August, and there were thirteen days left until the auction sale. Tucking the tin box full of treasure under his arm, he headed for home, with Johnny and Sam trailing after him.

Mrs. Paine smiled too when she heard the good news. So did the man in New York whom she went to see the next day. He was in the business of buying and selling old letters and pictures and books. He knew all about Washington's spies and Samuel Morris.

"He says the Woodruff letters are the find of the century," Nat proudly reported to Jim and the girls. "He's going to sell them for us and give us the money."

"Thousands and thousands and thousands of dollars," Sam interrupted. "We're going to be *rich*."

"Not rich." Johnny corrected him with a frown. "But we'll have enough to pay the taxes and —"

"And maybe Mr. Dean will buy the letters and give them to York University and —" Nat continued.

"Who's he?" Pat nudged Barbara.

"Owns that baking company out at the far end of Main Street," Barbara whispered back. "Loaded with money."

"That way the letters will stay in Haven, and they'll be the Nathaniel Woodruff Collection," Nat finished.

Before the summer was over, Mr. Dean did buy the letters and did give them to the university library. A lady photographer drove up from New York to take pictures of the collection and of the Paine boys in the house that Great-grandpa Woodruff had built so long ago. There was a new pane of glass in the kitchen window, a new furnace in the cellar, and every single brick in all of the fireplaces was solidly cemented into place.

It would be nice to report that everyone lived happily ever after, but that isn't the way things happen, except in fairy tales. Nat kept on being bossy and yelling at the girls whenever they played baseball. Barbara was still a shrimp who talked too much, and Pat never did learn to climb up the oak tree without a big boost from below.

After school started in September, however, Pat found that she had learned at least one useful lesson during the long summer months. When she passed a note across the aisle to Barbara or along the row to Jim, her teacher might confiscate the note but she couldn't read it. Neither could any of the other boys and girls in the class. That was because the note said things like "12-6 3-5 15-7 5-16." That was because the note was in code, and only Pat and Barbara and Jim knew that the key to the code lay in the sixth grade's new green spelling book.

NATHANIEL WOODRUFF was invented for this story, but there really was a Secret Service during the American Revolution which operated in New York City, on Long Island, and in Westchester County, New York. Responsible directly to General Washington or his aide, Major Tallamadge, the spies used false names, alphabet and number codes, and even invisible ink. You can find out more about them in *George Washington's Spies*, by Morton Pennypacker. You might also like to read *Codes and Secret Writing*, by Herbert Zim, the book that Barbara refers to on page 128.